Lord Alistair Stewart not only shadowed every dazzling London ball that Honaria attended, he now had destroyed her precious solitude as she danced alone beneath the trees in a London park.

"*You*," she said, when she saw his tall, superbly attired figure and his handsome, mocking face.

"Yes, come to take the glory out of the morning for you. Why the merry dance? Does the memory of Lord Channington lend your feet wings? Go carefully there, Miss Honeyford. Channington pursues 'em and woos 'em, but never, ever, does he marry 'em."

"Just like yourself," said Honaria coldly.

"No, not just like myself. To put it crudely, I leave their virginity intact."

Bright color flamed in Honaria's face—and a chill ran through her. What if this man who spoiled everything was right—and she faced ruin if she were wrong. . . ?

The Original
Miss Honeyford

SIGNET Regency Romances You'll Enjoy

The Original Miss Honeyford

Marion Chesney

A SIGNET BOOK

NEW AMERICAN LIBRARY

SIGNET TRADEMARK REG. U.S. PAT. OFF. AND FOREIGN COUNTRIES
REGISTERED TRADEMARK—MARCA REGISTRADA
HECHO EN CHICAGO, U.S.A.

SIGNET, SIGNET CLASSIC, MENTOR, PLUME,
MERIDIAN AND NAL BOOKS
are published by New American Library,
1633 Broadway, New York, New York 10019

First Printing, May, 1985

1   2   3   4   5   6   7   8   9

PRINTED IN THE UNITED STATES OF AMERICA

For Abner Stein,
with love

One

It would be a long time before Honoria Honeyford, Honey to her family and friends, could
forgive Amy Wetherall. Up until the day Amy
and her family arrived to take up residence in
the town of Kelidon, Honey had ruled the roost.

All the gentlemen of the neighborhood called
on Honey and seemed to enjoy her easy, infor-
mal company. Honey had not had to endure
any of the boring social training of a future
debutante. Instead of studying the use of the
globes, the Italian language, watercolor paint-
ing, music, and how to handle a fan, she learned
Greek and Latin, mathematics and science, and
read the works of every radical writer she could
get her hands on. Her favorite book was Mary
Wollstonecraft's *Vindication of the Rights of
Women*. She insisted in conversing with men
on equal terms, and in wearing comfortable,
mannish clothes. Her hair was cut as short as
Caroline Lamb's, and the townspeople prophe-

sied that the beautiful Miss Honeyford would soon become just another country eccentric.

For Honey *was* beautiful. What she had of her hair after her ruthless shearing was thick and shiny, a rich chestnut color highlighted with threads of gold. She had a trim figure, and a small, elfin face with wide hazel eyes and thick black lashes.

Had her mother been alive, things might have been different, but widower Sir Edmond Honeyford spoiled his headstrong daughter, and, perhaps, was just a little guilty of trying to turn her into the son he had always wanted. Honey was an expert shot, skilled in the use of the small sword, and upset the local hunt by riding to hounds and cheerfully copying the language of the lowest of the grooms.

Honey was amused and curious when she first heard of Amy Wetherall's arrival in the district. Sir Edmund laughed and said Amy must be a diamond of the first water because all the young fellows professed themselves shot by Cupid's arrow. Being curious to see the fair Amy himself, he accepted invitations to a musical soirée at the Wetherall home for himself and Honey.

The Honeyfords lived in a large, square barracks of a mansion on the outskirts of Kelidon. The servants were all men and Honey scorned the services of a lady's maid, so the house looked more like a gentlemen's club and smelled of brandy and woodsmoke and the cheroots that Honey and her father smoked when they were conversing of an evening.

When they set out for the Wetheralls', Sir Edmund was neatly if unfashionably dressed in an old chintz coat and knee breeches. Honey was wearing a round gown in a depressing shade of mud brown. Her only ornament was an enormous cameo brooch that showed a heavy-featured Roman matron who looked as if she had just seen another Christian thrown to the lions.

The spring night was cold and so Honey wore a heavy, many-caped garrick over her gown. She paused for a moment before putting it on, because her two pet foxhounds, who were allowed the run of the house, had been using it for a bed and it smelled abominably of damp dog, but she reassured herself with the thought that she would not be wearing the garrick during the soirée. Her gown was un-fashionably long and reached the floor, so it seemed silly to wear thin silk slippers on such a cold night and Honey pulled on a comfort-able pair of half boots.

The Wetheralls had taken the late squire's estate on the other side of Kelidon. They drove through the market town, both of them sitting up on the box. Honey was driving the team of four horses and she set too fast a pace through the town for safety, but Sir Edmund enjoyed his daughter's skill with the reins, and was proud of saying that she could drive to an inch, and so he hung tightly onto the side, and happily watched the shops and houses whizzing by. He was a small, plump man who still wore his hair powdered despite the iniquitous flour tax. He had always been considered the real squire of Kelidon, even when Mr. Pembroke, the old squire, had been alive, for Mr. Pembroke had been a thin, scholarly man, quite the opposite of the jolly, sports-loving Sir Edmund.

Sir Edmund had indulged Honey's every whim. He often fondly remembered the day she had rebelled against her governess, demanding a "real" tutor instead. Not a bookish man himself, Sir Edmund nonetheless admired his daughter's capacity for devouring literature. Lady Honeyford had died when Honey was only six and so there had been no feminine restraint on Honey's eccentric upbringing.

So there they were on a fine spring evening with the new leaves turning the trees into clouds of black lace in the moonlight, as contented and happy a father and daughter as could be found in the whole of England in this year of 1812. But that was before they met Amy Wetherall.

The squire's house had been a rambling, ivy-covered building, famous for its wilderness of garden, its bad drains, and its gloomy rooms. As they approached it up the now-well-tended drive, both noticed that the ivy had been stripped off, the bricks repointed, and that a smart new portico had been built over the entrance.

Lights blazed from every window and all the curtains had been drawn back as was the fashion in faraway London when someone was having a rout.

Honey found herself hoping that she could divest herself of her garrick before anyone other than the butler saw it.

But other guests were arriving at the same time, and as Honey entered the hall, one young miss said loudly, "I did not think the Wetheralls kept dogs indoors. There is the most monstrous smell of damp hound."

Honey found that she was expected to leave her garrick in a room set aside for the ladies' cloaks. She quickly got rid of it by tossing it behind a screen. Other ladies were primping in front of the looking glass. Honey knew them all, but none of them greeted her with any warmth for Honey preferred the company of men and had been unwittingly very rude to all these local ladies in the past. She noticed how finely dressed they all were that evening. Her own reflection gazed back at her, a drab figure set against all the pretty pastel muslins and silks. When the old squire had entertained, the house had been dreadfully cold, but that night it was warm. It was not only the heat from the fires which had been lit in every room—not wood fires either but great, blazing conflagrations of sea coal—but also the heat from hundreds of the finest beeswax candles.

In the squire's day, the rooms had been shadowy and dim. Now Honey felt as if she were standing on a stage. She saw dog hairs clinging to the wool of her gown and nervously brushed them off. Perhaps sensing that his daughter might find herself uneasy in such new, tonnish surroundings, Sir Edmund had waited for her in the hall.

He blinked a little as she emerged from the cloakroom, seeing her clearly for the first time, seeing the short, short hair and the dowdy gown. Her hem caught against a chair, and before she pulled it down, Honey had shown her father and the company that she was wearing cracked half boots and darned green stockings.

Sir Edmund tugged at the lapels of his chintz coat and wished for the first time in his life that he had gone to the trouble of having a new evening coat made.

A music room had been built onto the back

of the house, and a famous soprano called Madame Venuti was to entertain them. No one had heard of her before, but the magnificence of the Wetherall home went a long way toward persuading them that they must have read about her some time or another.

Mrs. Wetherall was waiting at the door of the music room to receive her guests. She was a thin, spare woman with iron-gray hair confined under a lace cap. She had pale, rather protruding gray eyes and strong yellow teeth which she displayed as much as possible.

Mr. Wetherall was a large, sagging man with a sallow face, who, it was rumored, had made his money in India.

And then there was Amy Wetherall.

Honey was slim and slight in stature, but Amy Wetherall made her feel like a great lumering ox, for Amy was positively ethereal in a gold tissue gown. Her brown hair was artistically dressed in disarrayed curls, and their shine owed all to good health and nothing to pomatum. She had very large, pansy-brown eyes, a rosebud mouth, and a neat, straight nose. Her gown was cut low at the bosom and a double row of pearls shone against the whiteness of her neck.

Honey curtsied to all the Wetheralls, trying by the elegance of her curtsy to offset the dowdiness of her gown. The music room was only a few yards away, but it seemed like miles to the self-conscious Honey. She was grateful to sink down in a chair at the back, next to her father, and feel the embarrassed flush beginning to die out of her cheeks. The musical performance was agony for Honey. The soprano had a shrill, penetrating voice and sang slightly off-key, but was warmly applauded by the other guests, who equated culture with excrutiating agony and, therefore, considered Madame Venuti a diamond of the first water.

Following the concert, everyone moved into a pretty flower-bedecked saloon for supper, and there was a great deal of laughing and jostling as the men vied with each other for a place next to Amy. Honey watched Amy covertly from under her lashes. Amy flirted to a nicety, waving her fan with delicate little motions of her wrist, and laughing a silvery, tinkling laugh.

Can't they see everything she does is an act? thought Honey. I shall *never* become like that. I treat all men as equals. She looked about for some man to treat as an equal but, old and young, they were all clustered about Amy.

"I hear you are going to London, Miss Wetherall," said a young officer. "You will break all hearts there as you have done here."

Amy peeped up at him over the barrier of her fan. "Captain Jocelyn, I cannot believe the

gentlemen of London will be any more charming than the gentlemen of Kelidon. Faith! Can
you see me in Hyde Park on the arm of some
Bond Street fribble?" Amy put down her fan,
felt at the side of her face as if feeling side
whiskers, and said in a gruff voice, "Pon rep,
Miss Weatherall, your gown is almost as well
cut as my coat, and, damme, if your *reticule*
does not match my waistcoat!"

There was a great burst of hearty masculine
laughter. Honey saw to her amazement that
one of the gentlemen laughing the loudest was
her father, and yet she felt Amy had said nothing that was witty, clever, or even funny.

One gallant finally succeeded in being favored with a seat next to Amy, and the rest of
the gentlemen dispersed to find other seats.
Captain Jocelyn sat down beside Honey in an
absent-minded way, his eyes still on Amy.

At last he reluctantly turned his attention to
Honey. "Ah, Miss Honeyford," he said, "you
must forgive me. My thoughts were elsewhere."

Captain Jocelyn was a very handsome man
with a strong, tanned face and steady gray
eyes, home on leave from the Peninsular Wars.
Honey had already met him on the hunting
field and considered him a very superior sort
of gentleman.

All at once, Honey wanted him to listen to

her as intently as he had been listening to Amy.

"Captain Jocelyn," she began, "I would like your opinion on the Regent's wider powers. Do you think he will make a coalition government? He has suggested the idea to the Chief of Whigs, but it is said that Percival does not care for the idea of a coalition. Do *you* think it a good thing?"

At that moment, Amy's silvery laugh rang out. She leaned forward and said something to her partner. Captain Jocelyn bent a little way away from Honey, straining his ears, obviously hoping to catch what Amy was saying.

At last he turned back to Honey with an obvious effort. "I am sorry, Miss Honeyford," he said. "You were saying. . . ?"

Blushing slightly, Honey repeated the question. Captain Jocelyn had always been eager to discuss politics with her before. Now he said, "I do not know, Miss Honeyford. The deuce! Have you ever seen such eyes?"

Now this was no doubt the kind of remark he would have made had he been talking on equal terms with another man, but Honey felt piqued. "Miss Wetherall is very beautiful, is she not?" she remarked, trying for a free and easy manner.

"Very beautiful," said Captain Jocelyn dreamily. "You're a good sort of chap, Miss Honeyford.

You know what I mean. Only see the delicate turn of her wrist and the sparkle in her eyes. She makes a fellow feel ten feet tall."

Honey winced at that "good chap," forgetting that before this evening she would have considered it a very fine compliment. "I hope Miss Wetherall has an informed mind to match her beauty," said Honey.

"Oh, Miss Wetherall is extremely clever," said the captain. "She drew a picture of Lady Jenkins' cocker spaniel and it was that dog to the life. She embroiders exquisitely, and her voice! She sings like an angel."

Honey felt at a loss. She wanted to jump up and down, and say, "Look at me! *I'm* a woman."

"Does Miss Wetherall hunt?" she asked desperately.

"Gad, no! Too much of a lady to do that. I shudder to think of such a delicate angel riding out with us coarse fellows. It don't bear thinking of."

"*I* hunt, as you very well know, Captain Jocelyn," said Honey crossly.

He appeared to see her for the first time that evening. As he glanced at her, Honey became aware again of the dowdiness of her gown, and put a nervous hand up to her cropped curls.

"So you do," he said indulgently, "but one don't think of *you* as a lady, Miss Honeyford. I mean to say, don't notice the difference on the hunting field. Lord, it made me laugh t'other day when old Harry Blenkinsop said you swore worse than his head groom." Captain Jocelyn laughed heartily.

Honey felt herself diminishing in size before his loud laughter. She felt if she became any smaller then she might disappear altogether.

The supper room was very hot and very scented. The other ladies were wearing the thinnest of muslins. Honey's gown felt scratchy and prickly against her skin.

After supper was finally over, Honey looked to her father, hoping he would say it was time to go home. But Mrs. Wetherall announced that the chairs had been cleared in the music room and that they were going to have an impromptu dance. Everyone, except Honey, hailed the news with delight. Gloomily, she watched Captain Jocelyn dashing off without even a fairwell to see if he could persuade Amy to dance with him.

Bleakly, Honey sat with the dowagers in the music room while couples began to form sets for a country dance. She felt very much the wallflower and moved away to sit behind a pillar.

"I'd better find someone to dance with," came a man's voice from the other side of the pillar. "John Anderson," thought Honey. John and she were great friends. If she stood up and walked around the pillar, surely he would ask her to dance.

"Too late to get the fair Amy," said another voice. "I saw your friend Miss Honeyford a moment ago. Why not ask her?"

A tremulous smile on her lips, Honey half rose from her seat. "Oh, not *her*," said Mr. Anderson with dreadful clarity. "Fact is, she goes on like a man and, damme, she would probably *lead*. Good sort but hardly . . . well, *you* know."

Their voices faded as they moved away.

Honey sat like a stone. She *hated* Amy Wetherall. These men had been her friends. She had enjoyed the warmth of their companionship. Now Amy, with her silly, flirty ways, had spoiled it all.

The music room disappeared momentarily in a blur of tears. Then Honey blinked them furiously away. Amy would shortly be leaving for London and then things could return to normal again. Would her father never come? It was unlike him to want to stay anywhere so late. But it was two in the morning before Honey was able to climb up into her father's carriage and take the reins.

Sir Edmund seemed abstracted and did not say anything on the road home.

All Honey wanted to do was to put her aching, humiliated head down on the pillow and go to sleep. But no sooner were they indoors than Sir Edmund said, "I would like to talk to you about something important, Honoria, before you go to bed."

Honey's heart sank. He only used her proper name when he was worried or angry.

Then she brightened a little. To sit in front of the fire and drink brandy and smoke cheroots would take some of the bad taste of the evening out of her mouth.

But the first sign that tonight was not going to be as other nights started when Sir Edmund asked for the tea tray to be sent into the drawing room instead of the brandy decanter. He waited, motioning Honey to silence, until tea was served.

He looked at her long and gravely, and then he said, "I have made a sad mull of your upbringing. I would that your dear mama were alive."

"I have no complaints, Papa," said Honey, alarmed and anxious.

"No? Well, more's the pity. It should have been you tonight with all the gentlemen clustering around. It broke my heart to see you look . . . such a . . . *frump.*"

"Papa!"

"Yes, a frump, Honoria. I was ashamed enough of my own appearance. We have rubbed along together comfortably like two old bachelors, so comfortably that I had begun to forget you were a young lady of marriageable years."

"But there is nothing wrong with our life," said Honey. "We are happy."

"There's no going back. I thank the good Lord that you are young enough, and what has been done can be undone. You must be trained to become a lady, Honey, a lady of whom I can be proud."

"It's that wretched Amy," said Honey. "She has ruined everything. You were proud of me once."

"I still am, in a way. No, do not blame Miss Wetherall. One day you will thank her for raising the shutters from my eyes. Do you remember your aunt, your mother's eldest sister, Lady Canon?"

"Aunt Elizabeth. Yes, vaguely."

"Last year she wrote to me offering to be your chaperone during the London Season. I refused, saying you were too young, but, in truth, I wanted to keep you by me. This very night I am going to write to Lady Canon to sáy you will be traveling to London to join her."

"I cannot leave here," said Honey, beginning to cry. "Amy will be leaving soon and then we can be comfortable again."

"I can never be comfortable until I see you

married to a good man who will appreciate your fine qualities."

"But marriage! You have encouraged me to have an independent mind, to think for myself. Marriage means being a slave, tied at home, a lifetime of childbirth and illness!"

"Hush, child, you will come to long for marriage once you are away from my crude influence. It is no use crying, my child. My mind is made up."

"I shall go to London if you wish, Papa," said Honey, drying her tears. "But nothing, and no one, is going to turn me into a simpering, posturing miss like Amy Wetherall."

"I think love might do what I have failed to do," said Sir Edmund.

"Love! I will never love anyone, if by love you mean romantic love. It demeans a woman and turns her into a groveling lapdog, panting for the sound of the master's footstep."

"We'll see," sighed Sir Edmund. "Now leave me."

By the time Honey awoke the next morning, she had managed to convince herself that her father had had a kind of brainstorm.

And it did seem during the following week as if Sir Edmund had forgotten about the whole thing. But the young men who used to call to chat with Honey and Sir Edmund were conspicuously absent.

Honey decided at the end of the week to go for a long country walk to release the nervous energy which had plagued her since the Wetherall's party. She crammed a depressing beaver hat down on her curls and shrugged herself into her garrick, quite forgetting that she had sworn never to wear it again.

After she had walked several miles, she began to feel more relaxed and cheerful. She walked through the town, stopping to chat with various townspeople, and then, almost despite herself, she made her way out of the far end of the town toward where the Wetheralls lived.

"I am being very silly," she chided herself. "The gentlemen must be engaged in other pursuits, which is why they have been absent. They cannot be spending all of their time *spooning* Miss Wetherall."

As she rounded a bend in the road, the entrance to the Wetherall house was in front of her and there was a great commotion outside on the road as a carriage drew out. Every eligible man in the county was clustered around the gates. Amy Wetherall was leaving for London.

They were laughing and holding up gaily wrapped packages and flowers. The coach stopped and Amy stepped down into the roadway to receive her farewell presents.

Despite the chill of the day, she was wearing a round dress of fine French cambric under a pelisse of amber-shot sarcenet, ornamented with blue satin ribbons. Her Oatlands hat, which matched the pelisse, was tied with a checkered ribbon of blue on white and was surmounted with a bunch of tuberoses. Morocco shoes of light blue peeped out from below the fashionably short hemline. Long Limerick gloves were drawn up her arms to above the elbow, and her glossy brown curls were dressed forward on her forehead.

Honey turned and walked away quickly. She had long held the view that a lady should dress for comfort instead of being a hostage to fashion. But her own clothes now seemed simply eccentric. The gown she had worn to the musicale had been hot and scratchy. How much more sensible had been the loose, light muslins of the other female guests.

But by the time she returned home her spirits were quite restored. With Amy gone, life would return to its usual pleasant pattern.

The house looked dark and shabby. Why had she never noticed that before? Stuffed foxes glared down from glass cases in the hall and a huge stuffed pike was set over the fireplace. A wind had got up and moaned dismally in the eaves.

She saw for the first time what the young men of the district must have seen—this odd, dark, gloomy house with its frumpish daughter. She had a picture of the Wetherall's place, bright with flowers and candles, and Amy, charming and flirting, every movement delicate and studied.

The footman, George, who had just opened the door into the hall from the nether regions, looked more like a poacher than a footman. His livery started off well above the waistline, being of faded claret laced with silver, but from the waist down, he was dressed in stained moleskin breeches and a pair of Sir Edmund's old hunting boots.

"Master wants to see you in the library, Miss Honoria," he said.

Honey let him help her out of her garrick and then she went into the library where her father sat before a small, smoking fire. He had a letter in his hand.

"Sit down, Honoria," he said, and Honey's spirits plummeted at the sound of that "Honoria."

"I sent an express to Lady Canon, and she has done me the courtesy to reply by the same. She says she will be delighted to take you in hand as soon as possible. I told her in my letter that I would be sending funds so that you may have a grand London wardrobe."

"Oh, *need* I go, Papa? If I promise to go next year. . . ."

"There is a mercenary side to all of this," sighed Sir Edmund. "The truth is, I do not know how to manage the land to make a profit. These valuable documents called leases are binding on the landlord, but wholly inoperative on the tenant. Because the tenant farmers do not know how to manage the land either, and scorn all new improvements, they end up paying me half the rent they owed to my father. I am afraid the reputed honesty of the British farmer is a mere fiction. When I try to find what they have in pocket, they declare their capital is someone else's—their aunt's, uncle's or grandmother's—and so the rents stay very low. The rent once put down is very difficult to get up again when they continue to plead poverty, and my agent, John Humphries, is too lazy and easy-going.

"It would help to have another man in the family, a son-in-law. To put it bluntly, a son-in-law with money."

"But you should have told me this before," wailed Honey, aghast. "*I* could have studied agriculture and learned all the new improvements."

Sir Edmund sadly shook his head. "The farmers and John Humphries will not take orders from a mere girl."

"I *hate* being a girl," said Honey passionately. "I wish I had been born a boy."

"Your odd upbringing makes you think so," said Sir Edmund. "Honey, do not turn into a country bumpkin."

"Papa," said Honey, blushing. "You were wont to say I had a fine mind."

"And so you have, my child, which is why Lady Canon should find you teachable."

"But anyone can learn what girls like Amy Wetherall learn—to play, draw, sing, dance, make wax flowers, bead stands, do decorative gilding and crochet work. And what good is that? A man cannot profit by a woman who can only bead slippers."

"Nor can he profit by a young girl who knows Greek and Latin," said Sir Edmund dryly. "In your mother's day, any young girl was expected to know as much about housewifery as the servants. But you have not even been trained in that. Honey, it is a woman's role in life to marry and bear children."

"Unless she is lucky," said Honey, jumping to her feet and beginning to pace up and down. "I *despise* young ladies like Amy Wetherall."

"Odso? Then why so jealous of her?"

"I! Jealous? Of that ... that ... posturing, simpering miss?"

"Yes, jealous. Jealousy is the one character defect that everyone claims everyone else has except themselves. There is no need to become a simpering miss, and the man who would want a wife like that is not the son-in-law for me."

"I am being sent off to the Marriage Mart like a cow!"

"Like a very lucky young girl. Have you not passed by that vast new edifice in Kelidon that they nickname the Bastille? That, my dear, is the workhouse. Think of the young women in *there* before you start sulking over fine balls and fine company."

Tears sprang to Honey's eyes. "You are harsh, Papa."

"I am being deliberately harsh so that you will take your leave with better grace. For you leave tomorrow."

"I have made no preparation. I *cannot* leave tomorrow."

"But I have. You have little to pack since you have nothing that is suitable. The only thing that concerns me is that I have not been able to find a woman in the town who could act as a lady's maid."

"I have never had a maid. I do not need one."

"You will have two grooms and the coachman. But it is not fitting for a young lady of

Quality to stay at a posting house without a female companion."

"I am perfectly capable of managing on my own," said Honey.

"We will see. There is still a little time. Now go to your room and pack only the things you think will be suitable for London."

"What about Jasper and Casper?" Jasper and Casper were Honey's pet foxhounds.

"They will do to keep me company."

"Oh, Papa, why don't *you* come with me?"

"Because the two of us in London would be just too much expense. Please do not make it hard for me, Honey. You *must* go."

Honey went and knelt in front of him and looked pleadingly up into his face. "If I try very hard to dress prettily and look like a lady," she said, "then I might marry someone locally—perhaps like Captain Jocelyn."

He ruffled her short curls, and sighed, "No, my child. Captain Jocelyn and the others would still see the Honey of the hunting field. Do not tear my heart any longer with your pleas. You are going, Honoria, and that is that!"

Two

The servants who were to travel to London with Honey, that is, the coachman, Jem Judkin, and the two grooms, Peter Dasset and Abraham Jellibee, were more concerned with the niceties of fashion than was their mistress.

They complained their waistcoats had horizontal stripes and no decent coachman or groom wore *those*; only indoor servants wore *those*. Vertical stripes were the thing. They protested they could not appear in "Lunnon" looking countrified with such passion that Sir Edmund relented and delayed Honey's departure until new liveries could be run up by the three-shilling-a-day man. Since Honey was to be furnished with a new wardrobe in London, he quite forgot she might need new clothes for the journey, and so it was a very unfashionably young lady who at last took the road.

And yet Honey felt she had done her best. Under her gown of blue kerseymere, she wore a long linen corset and two petticoats. The very discomfort of her underwear convinced her that she was suffering to be fashionable since the length of the corset made it impossible to lounge, and the only way she could achieve any modicum of comfort was by sitting bolt upright. Over her gown, she wore a mantle of white bombazine, and, on her head, a cavalier hat ornamented with a rather tired-looking ostrich feather.

She bade her father a tearful farewell and set out on the road to London.

The spring weather was fine. The new wheat formed a green haze over the fields. The long line of Lombardy poplars at the edge of the six-acre field showed their new leaves, more yellow than green, giving the trees an odd autumnal air. The flowering spikes of the horse chestnuts stood up proudly against a pale blue sky. Coots were quarreling beside the village pond, and the first bluebells were growing in patches in the woods. Small white butterflies performed their zig-zag dance over the early bracken.

Skylarks were rising straight up from the fields until they were mere dots against the sky, sending down burst upon burst of song.

Everything was new, fresh, and bustling. With the resilience of youth, Honey dried her eyes and began to look forward instead of back.

If she did not manage to find a husband, it would not be so very terrible. They would manage somehow. They had always managed in the past.

But, then, there just *might* be a husband waiting for her, a man perhaps like Captain Jocelyn, or, rather, as Captain Jocelyn had been before the arrival of Amy.

So Honey dreamed the first day's journey away, thinking of some man with whom she could share the winter evenings, the two of them on either side of the fire, drinking brandy and smoking cheroots, not realizing she only wanted someone like her father, only wanted things to be as they had always been.

Honey was glad her father had not been able to find a maid to accompany her. How much pleasanter to dream without being interrupted by some silly female.

She had only been as far as twenty miles from Kelidon before. Then she had gone to a large cattle market with her father. She remembered with amusement the coaching inn called The Blue Boar. She certainly did not need the company of some lady's maid to give her ton at any such English hostelry.

She remembered their meal being interrupted by the arrival of the coach. The passengers who traveled inside were very conscious of their superiority, and no "outsider"—the ones who traveled on the roof—would dream of finding a seat at the table before the insiders were seated. The coach passengers were only allowed half an hour to eat, and most complained bitterly about the menu, which was made up of pork in various shapes, roast at the top, boiled on the bottom, sausages on one side, fried bacon on the other. Then the coachman, a large strong-smelling man in a mountainous greatcoat, indicated with a bob of his head and a sort of waltzing motion of his hand behind his back that tipping time had come. The passengers had barely time to eat before they were shrugging themselves back into their husks, accompanied by dives into pockets and reticules for the needful, and everyone wondering how little he could tip without getting a snubbing from the coachman. Then a monstrous cry of, "All right! Sit tight!" was heard, showing that the coach was out on the road again. Hardly a tonnish scene, thought Honey. Putting on airs would be a waste of time.

But, until this journey, Honey had never stayed at a really good posting house, and her heart sank a little as The Magpie hove into view.

It was a modern building with a glistening white portico and glossy green shutters. There was a very fine traveling carriage being led around to the stables, and, in the light of the big oil lamp that swung over the inn door, Honey could make out a crest on the panels.

Her servants were so used to Miss Honoria's taking charge, that, once they had seen her safely deposited in the hall of the posting house, they went off to the stables to make arrangements for the new team to be harnessed in the morning.

Honey looked about her nervously, at the bright fire in the hall crackling before the solid brass fender, at the polished floorboards, and then at the very superior individual in black knee breeches and a swallowtail coat who turned out to be the manager.

The manager explained he had set up a truckle bed in Miss Honeyford's room for her maid, and raised his thin eyebrows superciliously when she explained she had not got one.

He eyed Honey's clothes with a quick, practiced glance. Honey defiantly turned away from him and straightened her hat in the long mirror on one side of the hall. She blushed as she saw that Jasper's and Casper's enthusiastic farewell had left its mark—or marks. On the white of her bombazine coat were four black paw prints.

"Have my bags taken upstairs," said Honey, turning around, "and show me to my room."

The manager turned and walked upstairs, presenting to Honey's gaze the most insolent-looking pair of shoulders she thought she had ever seen. It was as well, she thought ruefully, that Papa had bespoke her room at this inn by sending a letter by the mail coach, otherwise, she felt sure, the supercilious manager would have turned her from the door.

The room was better appointed than most country house bedchambers. There were pretty rose and white chintz curtains at the window and the bed hangings were of the same design. Brass-bound cans on the toilet table held piping hot water, and there were two unused cakes of Joppa soap.

Honey dismissed the manager after he had told her supper would be laid for her in the dining room as soon as she cared to put in an appearance. His manner was a little more polite. Honey was used to giving orders and her self-confidence had been restored by the comfort of the room.

She changed her gown for a dark brown silk of old-fashioned cut after having sponged her face and combed her hair. She consoled herself with the thought that they were not yet on the main London road, and so, with any luck, she would have the dining room to herself.

The very quietness of the posting house added to this hope as she went down the stairs. There were no noisy voices resounding from the tap. It was easy to find the dining room because each room had its sign in curly letters over the door.

Honey bumped into a chair which was awkwardly placed just inside the door, and, being under the impression that the dining room was empty, she relieved her feelings by cursing loudly.

"No, no, no," urged a gentle voice. "Pray don't swear, ma'am. Spoils the shape of the mouth."

Honey, who had bent down to straighten the chair, jerked upright and stared.

Lit by two tall candles placed on a small table by the bay window sat a gentleman. As Honey stared, he took out his quizzing glass and calmly surveyed her from head to foot.

Honey flushed and put up her chin. Lord Alistair Stewart dropped his glass and gave her a bewitching smile.

Then he blinked and his heavy lids came down to veil the expression in his blue eyes. For Lord Alistair, youngest son of the Duke of Bewley, was not used to being viewed with just that gleam of contempt that he had caught in the hazel eyes which were studying him from the doorway. He gave an infinitessimal shrug and poured himself another glass of wine. It did not really matter what some country schoolgirl miss with an outlandish coiffure and a dowdy dress thought of him.

Totally unaware that she was being very rude, Honey continued to stare. He was everything, she decided, that she detested in a man. He was too tall, too handsome, too indolent. From his guinea-gold hair to his gleaming hessian boots stretched out under the table, he was an exquisite example of expert valeting and Weston's tailoring. A large sapphire ring flashed on one of his long white fingers. His cravat rose in snowy folds to a strong chin. His mouth was well-sculpted, but his blue eyes were lazy, and he looked, in fact, just the kind of man who would call simpering misses like Amy Wetherall "adorable," thought Honey, forgetting that all the men in Kelidon had thought Amy adorable.

"Beg pardon, ma'am," drawled Lord Alistair, "but didn't your mama ever tell you it was rude to stare?"

"I am sorry," she said stiffly. She looked about her for a table, and saw to her dismay that the only other table that was laid for supper was next to the lazy gentleman's on the other side of the bay.

The gentleman had obviously finished dinner, for the cover had been removed and a decanter of port, a bowl of walnuts, and a bowl of fruit were reflected in the gleaming mahogany of the table.

Honey sat down, stared resolutely at the

drawn curtains over the window, and waited. And waited. At last, she got to her feet and rang the bell, every movement feeling stiff and awkward as she was aware of the gentleman's eyes on her.

Another long time passed. Lord Alistair took pity on her. He rose languidly to his feet and sauntered to the door, opened it, and shouted loudly, "Waiter!" He strolled back and a waiter erupted into the room at his heels.

"Serve the lady," said Lord Alistair, and returned to his port.

Soon Honey was served with mulligatawny soup followed by wine-roasted gammon and sweetbreads *"à-la-daub."* She ordered a bottle of Teneriffe and then turned stiffly to the tall gentleman. "I thank you sir," she said gruffly. "Without your help, I might not have been served."

"Think nothing of it, ma'am," he said lazily. "Fact is, I had to do something about it. You see, I could have wanted something and so I share the insult."

Honey could really think of nothing to say to this, and so she merely inclined her head and then concentrated on finishing her meal as quickly as possible.

But she gradually felt bolder after drinking most of the wine, and decided to ring for brandy. The waiter jumped to its summons this time. The cloth was removed and the brandy, fruit, and nuts placed before her. She searched in her reticule and brought out her cheroot case, extracted one, and turned to her companion of the dining room. "Your permission, sir?"

He nodded, a flash of amusement in his blue eyes, and somehow Honey knew that *he* knew she was well aware that young ladies did not smoke cheroots in a public dining room—or anywhere else for that matter—and was only doing it as an act of bravado.

"You are very young to be traveling alone, ma'am," he said.

"I am not alone," said Honey. "I have my coachman and two grooms."

"But no maid or female companion?"

"Sir," said Honey patiently, "you have reminded me of my manners this evening and now it is my turn to remind you of yours. We have not been introduced."

"Easily remedied," he said, rising to his feet and making her a bow. "Lord Alistair Stewart, bell-ringer and waiter-caller, at your service."

"I am Miss Honeyford," said Honey in a flat sort of let-us-finish-this-conversation-now voice.

"There you see, now we are acquainted. Are you fleeing the seminary, Miss Honeyford?"

"I am nineteen years, my lord, and no schoolgirl. What on earth gave you the impression I was fresh from the seminary?"

"The cheroot," he said, waving his quizzing glass to and fro on its long gold chain. "It makes you look like a naughty schoolgirl."

"On the contrary, my lord, I often smoke cheroots of an evening when I am cozing with my father."

He raised his thin eyebrows and relapsed into silence.

"*And* drink brandy," added Honey defiantly.

"And swear as you did when you entered the dining room?" he asked at length.

"I did not know there was anyone here. I am not in the habit of swearing—except on the hunting field."

"So you hunt, Miss Honeyford."

"Yes," said Honey with a toss of her curls. "I like it above all things. You hunt yourself, of course."

"No, I have no taste for it."

"I thought not," said Honey, looking at him with contempt.

"Not the fox. I have hunted with the harriers. I looked very fine in my scarlet coat."

"You do not wear your pinks to hunt the hare," said Honey loftily.

"Ah, yes, that I discovered to my mortification. There I was, a veritable advertisement for Asher. And there *they* all were, all the myrtle-green gentlemen in their white cords, or twilled fustian frocks. Tell me, do you enjoy the kill?"

"Yes," muttered Honey, looking down at her lap. In fact, since the day she was first blooded, she had not stayed for the kill, being unable to bear it. But it seemed such a *womanish* thing to confess to.

Honey enjoyed hunting simply because of the hard riding involved and because it put her on easy terms with the men.

"You are not by any chance traveling to London, Miss Honeyford?"

"Yes, I am to make my come-out."

"I can see you now at Almack's, swearing like a trooper as you fall over Lady Jersey's train." He looked at her dress. "You will need to become a trifle more modish."

"I am to have a fine wardrobe when I reach London," said Honey, putting her chin up. "It is not necessary to wear fine clothes in the country."

"You surprise me. There are more gentlemen, Miss Honeyford, trapped into marriage at a country house than ever ran into the snare during the Season."

"I am only going to stay with my aunt to enjoy the pleasures of the metropolis. *You* do not hunt the fox because you have no taste for it. For the same reason, *I* do not hunt a husband."

"Perhaps just as well," he mocked. "We men are sadly old-fashioned, and a lady who hunts, drinks brandy, and smokes cheroots might be considered too intimidating."

"Not to a man of honesty and integrity."

"Ah, so you *do* have hopes."

"Yet that is not my sole reason for going," said Honey, wondering if this tall, elegant gentleman could read her mind, could see her pleading father and hear his request to bring home a son-in-law with money who would help to manage the land. She had a sudden picture of arriving home with this elegant, lazy fop, and grinned, a gamin grin which made her look like a cheeky schoolboy.

"Yes, you are quite right." He smiled. "We would not suit."

"I never even contemplated such a thing," said Honey.

"No, but you thought it, and a rare joke you thought it too."

"My dear sir, if I may say so without offense, you are a trifle too old for someone of my tender years and so the thought never even entered my head."

"Very true. I am thirty and that is a great age. But I still have all my own teeth."

"Do the ladies examine your teeth before

they contemplate entering matrimony with you? It sounds like a horse fair."

"They have no chance to contemplate any such thing. I have so far successfully escaped the parson's mousetrap."

"My lord, you are boasting. One would think all the ladies in society were storming your doors."

"Well, sometimes it does seem a little like that. It is not my charm or my looks they desire, but my title and fortune."

"Are you rich?" asked Honey.

"Very."

"Oh." Honey scowled ferociously into her now empty brandy glass. She wondered what it would be like to be very rich, and, at the same time, it hit her with force that her father was relying on her to bring home a husband, that they were desperately in need of money. She did hope all the marriageable gentlemen were not like this lazy lord. But there would no doubt be some military gentlemen like Captain Jocelyn. Her face brightened.

Lord Alistair watched the changing moods on her expressive face with some amusement. He had never before in his life met any female, old or young, who was so little impressed by him. For the moment, he found the novelty refreshing, although he was sure that any extended period of time in this farouche child's company would bore him to tears.

"Are you not nervous at venturing so far alone?" he asked.

"I am not alone," said Honey. "As I have already pointed out, I have a coachman and two grooms."

"A young lady should not be left in a posting inn to her own devices—particularly a young lady who drinks brandy like water. There are some dangers on the road that even the best of servants would be at a loss to handle."

"Pooh, I am equal to anything."

"Anything?"

"Give me an example?"

He leaned back in his chair and smiled at her, a wicked, seductive smile. "Imagine if I decided to subject you to an excess of civility. You could, of course, scream, but who are the servants going to believe? You or me?"

"You, my lord."

He rose from his chair, looming large in the candlelight, his shadow running up to the rafters of the room. "So if I were to approach you—"

He broke off, and sat down abruptly. While he had been getting to his feet, Honey had been searching in her bulging reticule. He found himself looking at a neat pistol held steadily in one small hand.

"It would be silly to even ask you if you know how to use that," he said.

"Very silly," replied Honey, outwardly calm and inwardly shaken by that threatening wave of masculine sensuality which had emanated from him as he had stood up.

"And it is loaded?"

"Of course."

"What an extraordinary girl you are. I am sure you will set London by the ears."

Honey tucked the pistol away in her reticule and rose to her feet. "I bid you good night, my lord," she said. "I make an early start in the morning."

He rose to his feet again and made her a low bow. "I wish you every success during the Season, Miss Honeyford," he said. "Try not to frighten us poor gentlemen too much."

Honey turned and left the room.

Lord Alistair remained standing for several minutes after she had left, a quizzical smile on his face.

Honey soon plunged down into sleep—and straight into Lord Alistair's arms. He was holding her very tightly and his lips came down on hers in a searing kiss. She wanted that kiss to go on forever, and, when he released her, she cried out with loss.

Her own cry awoke her and for several moments she lay in bed, blushing all over, feeling she had been deliberately haunted. The last man in the world she wanted to hold in her arms was Lord Alistair.

She tossed and turned and slept in fits and starts for the rest of the night.

Lord Alistair was crossing the hall as she made her way down the stairs in the morning. He turned and looked at her and then swept off his hat.

Honey looked at him and blushed painfully. She mumbled something and fled outside to where her carriage was waiting.

She fervently hoped she would never see him again.

Her long journey during the next few days passed without incident. By dint of paying the inn servants their vails on her arrival at each posting house, she was ensured of prompt and willing service. Of course, on her departure, when it transpired there was no more largesse forthcoming, they were apt to turn surly, but there was little they could do by that time to make Honey feel uncomfortable.

At the end of the week, she met with a setback. On her arrival at The Green Dragon in Rawson in Bedfordshire, she was told there was no room for her. In vain did she plead that her father had sent her bookings for each posting house ahead with the mail coach. The landlord professed ignorance. The Green Dragon was full to bursting point, and it transpired there had been a prize fight near the town that very day. At last the landlord volunteered the information that the only hope she had of a bed that night was some six miles west on a minor road at The Boar's Head. Honey's coachman listened carefully to the directions and once more they were on the road with the light fast fading from the sky.

The last slanting rays of the sun eventually lit up the frontage of The Boar's Head as Honey's coach lurched around a muddy, rutted bend in the dreadful road.

It was so old and ill-kept that it looked as if it were about to fall down and become part of the surrounding countryside. In the last century, it had been a popular place, but due to subsidence, the road had proved unsafe for the great, lumbering stage coaches, and so the London road had moved six miles to the east, leaving it largely abandoned.

A fantastic jumble of chimneys loomed above the roof, and two oriel windows on the front made it look as if it were glaring down the road, wishing ill luck on the fickle travelers who had deserted it so long ago.

But on that night it had, perhaps, a more cheerful view. Three men, travelers like Honey who had been unable to find an inn in the town, could be seen moving between the inn and the stables.

The rooms, in the old tradition, had names instead of numbers—Rose Parlor, Cliff Parlor, Crown Chamber, Key Chamber, and Moon Chamber. The landlord looked like a small tenant farmer with his large groggy face and bovine stare. His wife looked like his twin, and her broad hips in their voluminous skirts brushed either side of the stairway as she conducted Honey up to the Moon Chamber.

The room was fireless and damp, and the towels used by the last inhabitant had been merely dried, rather than washed, and put back again complete with brandy smell and snuff stains.

Honey became weary of all her independence. She stuck her head out of the window which overlooked the stable yard, and, seeing the groom, Abraham Jellibee, crossing the yard, she hailed him and told him to get fresh towels and hot water.

Then she sank down into an upholstered chair, which sent up a cloud of dust, and contemplated the legend carved on the mantel:

As trusting of late has been my sorrow
Pay me today and I'll trust you tomorrow.

At length Abraham arrived with towels and hot water, grumbling that it was unbecoming to his livery to act as an inn servant.

"Then find a servant," snapped Honey, exasperated.

"Don't seem to have one 'cept a poor lass that's mazed in the head and a liddle boy. Seems you must dine in the coffee room, miss, the roof of the dining room having fallen in this age."

"There are private parlors!"

"Them's into rooms for us grooms and such. Better I stand behind your chair tonight. There's a mort o' loud johnnies in the tap."

"And have you grumbling about being a waiter? Besides, you will be dining there yourself."

"Begging your parding, but Jem and Peter's for taking the carriage into town."

"What is the matter with it?"

"Don't rightly understand, but Jem said as how it was a liddle thing, and besides we could fare better in the town for victuals."

"Leaving me here to take pot luck?"

"Now, hasn't I just said as how I'd stay?" said Abraham with all the familiarity of an old country servant.

Honey bit her lip. She had coped very well on her own during the last week, but this was not a posting inn, and such company as there was would be gentlemen from the prize fight.

But a vision of Lord Alistair's sleepy blue eyes flashed before her. He had made her feel

young and silly, and he had had the imperti-
nence to haunt her dreams. She would show
him!

So, not stopping to consider that it was a
very sad thing to do—to go on trying to show
off to a man who wasn't even present—Honey
dismissed Abraham, who left after only a to-
ken protest, since he had had the foresight to
inspect the kitchens on his arrival.

Honey changed her dress, wondering what
would be served for supper. There had been a
cow grazing in the field next to the inn when
she had arrived. It looked like one of Pharaoh's
lean cattle and you could have hung your hat
on its hip bones. Doubtful if there would be
beef; probably pork. After some deliberation,
she tied a yellow, plush velvet poke bonnet on
her head. It gave her a rather blinkered view
of life, but she had worn it during the week
and found strangers inclined to ignore a female whose face was largely shut from sight.
She stuffed her pistol into her reticule, wondering at the same time whether she was being
missish by taking it with her for protection,
and the weight of it dragged on her arm.

Above the door of the coffee room was a sign:

This is a good world to live in,
To lend or to spend or to give in;
But to beg or to borrow or to get a man's own,
It's such a world as never was known!

Honey opened the door of the coffee room and walked in. Three gentlemen were seated at the top of a long deal table. Honey took a place at the bottom, showing her profile to the company so that nothing could be seen of her face, the hideous poke bonnet hiding it effectively. A brief glance at the young men before she sat down had shown her they were of the Corinthian persuasion since they were wearing Belcher neckerchiefs, loudly striped waistcoats, stuff coats, leather breeches, and top boots. Two of them lowered their voices as Honey took her place, but the third kept saying loudly, "Yarse. Yarse," and laughing inanely.

To Honey's amazement, she was served promptly, the main dish being chicken pie which was thumped down in front of her with great puffings and pantings and adjurations to "eat it while it's 'ot" by the landlord's wife. Even when the chicken proved to be rabbit and when the pastry reminded Honey obscurely of the day the roof at home had leaked and soaked the family Bible, she stoically ate as much as she could and prepared to make the best of things.

All three gentlemen had started talking loudly again. Their conversation was, mercifully for Honey, in too broad a cant for her to understand, and only by the frequent salacious laughs could she judge it was definitely not for the ears of a young lady. Not wanting to attract attention to herself, Honey did not call for her usual glass of brandy but contented herself with asking for canary instead. The landlady brought the wine, removed the dishes, and retired.

There was a lot of whispering and giggling from the three men, and then one said, "I say, miss or madam, we've been laying bets as to your age, not being able to see nothing with that *'straordinary* bonnet."

Honey pretended to be deaf and studied a gruesome picture of a dead dog on the opposite wall. Under it ran the legend, "Died last night, poor Trust! Bad pay killed him." This landlord, or the previous one, evidently wanted all his customers to understand he did not give credit.

Honey stiffened. There came the sound of chairs being scraped back. Then she relaxed. They were leaving.

But they stopped behind her chair.

Honey was just about to reach for her reticule, which was on the chair next to her, when a rough hand seized the poke of her bonnet and jerked the hat off her head. It was as well she had loosened the ribbons or she might have found herself dragged to the floor.

Three tipsy, weak faces stared down at Honey's upturned one.

"Gad! What a little beauty," said one with a face like a fox. "You should tell your mistress to give you better cast-offs, my maid."

"Go about your business, fellow," said Honey loftily, although she was trembling inside.

" 'Go about your business,' " mimicked the foxy-faced man.

"After we gets a kiss," leered another. He had a pockmarked face and, horror of horrors, his teeth had been filed to points.

Honey made a dive for her reticule, but her arms were clipped to her sides by the foxy-faced man, who pulled her to her feet and swung her around to face the other two. "Take your pleasure, boys," he said, "and then give me my chance."

Honey screamed loud and long.

"Quick," hissed Foxy Face, "before the landlord comes."

Honey struggled and kicked, but to no avail. Pockmarked Face grabbed her by the chin, and grinned down at her, his horrible pointed teeth winking in the light. His mouth descended toward hers. Honey screwed her eyes shut and prayed for help.

There was a tremendous crash as the door of the coffee room was thrown open.

The pockmarked one drew back with a curse, but Foxy Face still held Honey in a firm grasp.

Honey opened her eyes and gulped.

Lord Alistair Stewart stood on the threshold. "Let her go," he said mildly.

"There's three o' us," cried Foxy Face. "Up and at 'im!"

He released Honey, who scrabbled for her reticule. There was an enormous thumping and crashing. Honey knocked her reticule to the floor in her haste and with a moan of dismay dived under the table after it. The strings had tied themselves into a knot, and when she finally got them undone, she had to tear out a steel mirror, a tortoiseshell comb, a clean handkerchief, a book, and a netted purse, before she could get at the pistol, which had got itself wedged at the very bottom.

At last she succeeded in getting it out, and leaped up from under the table with a cry of triumph.

She blinked in amazement. Lord Alistair was leaning lazily against the door jamb, surveying her with amusement.

"My dear Miss Honeyford," he said. "This is the second time I find myself looking down the barrel of that pistol of yours and I find it unnerving to say the least."

"M-my l'lord," stammered Honey. "Those men! What happened?"

"They decided to lodge elsewhere."

The rattle of wheels from the courtyard outside followed his words.

"But there was a fight," said Honey.

"Yes, there was a little bit of a mill. It all happened while you were prudently hiding under the table."

"I was *not* hiding. My reticule had fallen to the floor when I was searching for my pistol." She retrieved the reticule and held it up.

His lordship raised his quizzing glass. "Dear me," he said languidly. "What a very large reticule. It could carry a pig. Excellent if you ever take to poaching."

"I made it myself," said Honey. "I despise the frippery things ladies usually carry."

"Ah, landlord," said Lord Alistair to the unseen figure behind his back. "You may find me a clean chamber and direct my man there with my traps. When you return, I will be most interested to learn why this lady was left without protection in this room. Her screams could be heard from here to Rawson."

"Oh, ah," said the landlord, shuffling off.

"I am delighted to learn you have some feminine traits, Miss Honeyford," said Lord Alistair, addressing himself to Honey again. "Your scream nearly lifted me out of the box of my carriage."

"Of course I screamed," said Honey. "I was shocked. I never would have dreamed that a lady could be attacked so in a public inn."

"I do not think they took you for a lady. I

think they were under the impression you were some sort of servant."

He walked past her and picked up her bonnet. "Were you wearing this?"

"Yes," said Honey, snatching it.

"There you are, then. Stands to reason they took you for a servant. I don't think I have ever seen quite such a repellent bonnet in my life."

"It was not repellent enough. Are you sure you are not hurt?"

"Yes, Miss Honeyford. Not a scratch."

"Oh, I suppose the banging and thumping I heard was the chairs falling over," said Honey, feeling disappointed, and wondering at the same time *why* she should feel disappointed.

"Chairs do make the most hideous racket," he said, picking up three of them and placing them back against the table. The landlord appeared in the doorway.

"Ah, landlord," said Lord Alistair. "Where am I?"

"In the Key," said the landlord. "Miss is in the Moon."

"So the moon *is* inhabited. That's one wager I have lost. Now, my good fellow, explain why you did not rush to aid Miss when she screamed."

"Wife says as 'ow she wus going to kill old pig at back. Same noise. Urr."

Honey giggled nervously, and Lord Alistair looked at her severely.

"Fortunately, I have dined," he said, "but bring us some brandy and port."

"I was just going to bed," said Honey.

"Nonsense. You may keep me company for a little."

Honey sat down weakly.

"I am surprised *you* did not obtain rooms in Rawson," she said. "Surely the crest on the panels of your carriage would have been enough."

He sighed. "You fatigue me, Miss Honeyford, and you will bore many men unless you learn to curb your tongue and control your passions."

"I am leaving," said Honey, getting to her feet.

"Bravo! I wondered how much more you could take."

Honey swept out and slammed the door behind her. Horrible, infuriating *fop*, she raged as she climbed the stairs to her room.

I was too hard, thought Lord Alistair. But I was only trying to be cruel to be kind. Such a babe is going to be hurt twenty times worse when she airs her views in London society.

But the room seemed dingy and empty without her. He had a picture of her wide, hurt, hazel eyes and her short chestnut curls standing up like an aureole about her head in the candlelight. He decided after long meditation that he had been unnecessarily rude. He would apologize to her in the morning.

When morning came, Lord Alistair found Honey had already left. His conscience bothered him. He had a desire to follow her. Then he shrugged. Miss Honeyford had a great deal of growing up to do, and any pursuit of her might appeal to her vanity and make her more outrageous than ever.

He noticed the morning, like his mood, was gray and flat, as if the departure of the stormy Miss Honeyford had taken all the color out of the day.

Three

Honey and her servants were now anxious to reach London. They stopped for only a few hours sleep at the next two posting houses on the road south. Honey would have been glad to have driven all night and all day in order to avoid another stop, but the horses had to be changed and the coachman and grooms were weary.

They decided to pass the night at The George in Barnet before pressing on to Lady Canon's in the West End of London in the morning.

By now Honey was used to grand posting houses and supercilious managers, and, after her stay at that terrible old coaching inn, The Boar's Head, she welcomed even the haughtiest of treatment.

She was a little intimidated when she entered the dining room to find it full of very grand people. She was glad she had saved her one fine gown, a sea-green silk of rather old-fashioned cut, for this last stop. She had washed and brushed her curls till they shone, and, fortified with her favorite book, *Vindication of the Rights of Women*, she asked to be given a table in a quiet corner, relieved that these modern posting houses had done away with the large communal dining table.

The meal was excellent, the company totally uninterested in her, and Honey was just beginning to enjoy herself when one of the ladies at the other end of the room exclaimed, "Lord Alistair! Can we hope this means your return to Town? This Season is sadly flat and full of counter-skippers and Cits."

"How sad," came Lord Alistair's amused voice. "I would have thought your presence, Mrs. Osborne, would have been society enough."

Honey glanced aross the room. Lord Alistair was joining a company of five richly dressed gentlemen and ladies at a table in front of the fire.

She lowered her eyes to her book again, but somehow she could not focus on the print. Everyone in the room seemed to be talking at once and so she could not hear what Lord Alistair was saying.

Six young men at a table near the window had been quarreling, not very loudly, but enough to cause an uneasy feeling in the room.

"Damn you, Giles!" yelled one, jumping to

his feet and oversetting a chair. "I demand satisfaction. Name your seconds."

"You are a card cheat and I stand by what I said, Jerry," said the one called Giles. "Tom and Billy will act for me."

"And Frank and Harry for me," said Jerry.

An old gentleman wearing a bag wig said loudly, "If you gentlemen insist on trying to kill each other, then I beg you to quit this room while you make your arrangements. You are frightening the ladies."

The six men rose from their seats, grumbling among themselves, and left the room. Everyone went on talking. Honey put down her book and sat amazed. Wasn't anyone going to *do* anything? Then she decided they probably knew the duel would come to nothing, and the six men were probably all drinking in the tap right at this moment.

She looked more openly at Lord Alistair, who appeared to see her for the first time. He gave her a small bow from the waist and turned his attention back to Mrs. Osborne, a dashing matron with a high complexion and brown curls topped with an outrageous bonnet which looked like a Roman helmet.

Honey felt disconcerted. There were three fashionably dressed ladies at Lord Alistair's table, including Mrs. Osborne. They all seemed to dote on him and hang on his every word.

But, somehow, Honey had thought he would pay her a little more attention. Feeling rather piqued, she got to her feet to leave the room. She could not help stealing a glance at Lord Alistair to see whether he was watching her leave, but he carried on talking.

A disgracefully feminine thought flashed through her head. "I am wearing my *best* gown and he didn't want to know me."

She entered her room and stared sulkily around the magnificence of Barnet's best posting house from the tasteful hangings to the framed landscapes and the Chippendale bureau and chairs.

Morosely, she undressed and went to bed. There was really nothing else to do.

Sleep came in fits and starts. Every time she decided she simply must get up instead of lying tossing and turning, she would plunge down into another fitful burst of sleep.

At last, she awoke properly at five o'clock in the morning. She decided to go for a short walk, got dressed, and opened the door of the old powder room which now served as a dressing room.

The one warm item she had was a sage-green cloak which had been her mother's. Honey had never worn it, considering its large hood and sweeping folds unsuitable for the country. It was, in fact, the most fashionable-looking item she possessed, the other few clothes that she had being the product of an elderly spinster dressmaker in Kelidon whose only other customers were the elderly ladies of the town. She was just adjusting it around her shoulders when she realized she could hear perfectly plainly what the two men in the next room were saying.

"I say, Frank," came a plaintive voice. "You don't s'pose old Giles is capable of *killing* Jerry, do you?"

The one called Frank gave a great horse laugh. "Giles is a fine shot, but he won't do any damage today. Fact is, Tom's sick and tired of Giles's moralizing and so he's only going to pretend to load Giles's pistol."

"But what if Jerry kills Giles?"

"Good riddance," came the laconic reply.

"Where do we meet?"

"The pasture on Hermitage Farm at a half past five. Just be getting light then. We've got time to walk there. Tom put it about that the duel was off. Don't want any of the stuffed shirts alerting the authorities."

Their voices faded as they walked to the door of their room.

Honey stood with her fists clenched. Something had to be done. She was well aware of the danger of interrupting six men at a duel in a lonely pasture at five-thirty in the morning.

Somehow, she must stop them without their knowing who had been responsible.

Two men in Kelidon, her father had told her, had once fought a duel over the old squire's daughter. She had stopped the duel, and her ungrateful gallants had not only railed at her but had gone out of their way to make her life a misery from that day on. Gentlemen were very peculiar about duels, Sir Edmund had said.

Honey only briefly contemplated enlisting the help of her servants. A servant interfering in a gentlemen's quarrel would have a sorry time of it.

There was, of course, Lord Alistair. But he would no doubt make nasty remarks about provincial schoolgirls leaping in where sensible members of the ton would know better than to tread.

Honey decided to find the pasture and then see if anything occurred to her. If Giles's seconds had been both loyal to him, she would have gone up to him and pointed out that his pistol was not loaded. But the very fact that his pistol would *not* be loaded proved them disloyal, and she might find herself facing five angry men, Jerry and the four seconds.

She let herself quietly out of the inn. Gold-edged bars of cloud were lying along the eastern horizon. Willow warblers sent down their tiny cascades of song from the birch trees. Yellow wagtails darted for flies among the spring grass.

Dogtooth violets were thick on the banks at either side of the road outside the inn, and comma butterflies sunned themselves on the stone walls, their closed ragged-looking wings like dead leaves.

Lord Alistair closed the casement window of his room. Now, just where was Miss Honeyford off to? He finished dressing and was just adjusting a small diamond pin in his cravat when he suddenly thought, "Dammit! The duel! The hen-witted female is out to stop it."

The duel was probably going to be held at that pasture at the Hermitage Farm which had become almost as famous a locality as Chalk Farm. Cursing Honey under his breath, he rushed down the steps and out of the inn door.

Meanwhile, Honey had reached the pasture, finding it by asking a countryman who was already out on the fields.

There was a thick windbreak of trees shielding the pasture from view. Honey climbed over the wall and made her way gingerly through the trees toward the sound of voices.

She came to a halt behind a large scrubby bush, and, crouching down, she looked around it. The antagonists had already chosen their weapons and the seconds were loading the guns—or, in the case of Giles's seconds, pretending to load.

Honey looked wildly up to the heavens, praying for a miracle. She saw a thick oak tree stretching its branches above her with one branch sticking well out over the field.

She crept back quietly to the base of the tree, and, taking off her hampering cloak, she folded it and laid it on the ground. Then, taking a deep breath, she began to climb, glad that she had left off her new corset. Nimbly she scaled the branches until she was stretched out on the branch over the field, hidden by the shifting and moving spring leaves.

Giles and Jerry now stood back to back. The handkerchief fluttered to the ground and they began to pace in opposite directions.

Honey remembered the games of "haunting" she had played with the children of the town on All Hallow's Eve when she was little. "Giles!" she called in a high, eerie voice. "Thou hast false friends. There is no ball in thy pistol."

Jerry's head snapped around. Giles stopped, his mouth open.

"I say," said Giles. "Did you hear that?"

" 'Twas nothing," said Jerry, but he had turned a muddy color with fright.

"It was the wind," said Tom.

"No harm in seeing," said Giles, looking about him strangely. He hefted the dueling pistol in his hand and then brought it down to the point. He frowned. "Doesn't feel as if there's a ball in it," he murmured. "Balance is wrong." He took off his hat and put it on the ground and fired the pistol into it. There was a flash, but when Giles picked up his hat and examined it, there was nothing to be seen but powder burns.

Very white in the face, Giles turned to face the others. "You murderers," he said coldly. Jerry raised his pistol and pointed it straight at Giles. Honey stuffed her knuckles in her mouth to stop herself from screaming. Giles whipped a steel Scottish pistol with a ramshorn butt out of his pocket. "*This* is primed. You fool, Jerry. Did you think I meant to kill you? Was that why you all cheated? But I will *now*, if you make a move."

"It was a mistake, Giles," gabbled Tom. "All a mistake, I swear. I was sure I loaded it. Let's forget about the whole thing and go back and talk it over at breakfast."

"You stay here and let me go my way on my own," said Giles bitterly. "I hope I never see any of you again."

Honey sighed with relief as Giles stalked off. The others waited uneasily and then burst out into recriminations and counterrecriminations, Jerry saying that he, Jerry, could not hit a barn door and that he had only intended to take Giles down a peg, each one trying to lie his way out of a plot that had gone wrong.

"But wasn't that voice from Heaven deuced odd?" he then said, narrowing his eyes—which made him look even more horrible, thought Honey, watching from her perch, for he had very mean-looking eyes already.

"I don't believe in strange voices," said Tom, all bluster and strut now that the danger was over. "It came from over there, I think."

And to Honey's dismay, he pointed straight at the tree in which she was hiding. All five men began to walk toward the tree. Honey shook with fear. They would find her cloak at the bottom of the tree and would soon begin to climb up after her.

But they had only gone a few yards when the field was suddenly filled with sheep. They seemed to appear out of the blue. They swept across the field in a great woolly mass, surrounding the men. Behind them came the shepherd.

The shepherd stopped and surveyed the men. Jerry quickly turned down the lapels of his coat, which had been turned up so that his white cravat would not afford an easy target.

"Been out for a walk," said Frank. "Let's go."

"I've a good mind to tell magistrate of what I seed," said the shepherd, his large eyes fixed on the long dueling pistol which Jerry still held in his hand.

"Now, now," said Frank heartily. "No need to bother the magistrate about a little bird-shooting, heh?" He pressed a sovereign into the shepherd's hand. The shepherd bit it, and then stowed it away in a pocket in his smock. He fixed them all with a bucolic stare. "Yes, as my friend was saying," said Tom, "no need to make a fuss. Here, my good man." Another sovereign found its way into the shepherd's hand.

The five shuffled out of the field, making their way carefully between the sheep.

Honey waited for a full ten minutes and then gingerly climbed down the tree, going very slowly because her legs were shaking.

She picked up her cloak and swung it about her shoulders.

"Thou hast surely sinned, Miss Honeyford," came a ghostly voice. "Interfere not in the sports of men."

Honey gave a gasp and the color drained from her face with fright. The voice had come from the other side of the tree. Honey was a firm believer in ghosts, but something forced her footsteps around the broad bole of the tree to see what demon was on the other side.

Lord Alistair was leaning negligently against the trunk.

"You!" said Honey in accents of loathing. "How dare you frighten me so! And how dare you stand there like a . . . a . . . *nothing*. You are a *man*. You should have done something."

"Ah, so there *is* something women cannot do. I must say, however, you coped admirably. I had quite a *frisson* when I heard that voice from the sky. How did you know that Giles's pistol was unloaded?"

"I overheard Jerry's seconds talking when I was getting my cloak out of the dressing room. They were in the next chamber. They said Tom was in on the plot. And it seemed as if Billy was faithless as well. Oh, all these Christian names! They seem so . . . so *familiar*."

"I doubt if you would want to know them any better," said Lord Alistair dryly. "May I escort you back to the inn?"

"Very well, since I am going there. It is all you are good for, Lord Alistair—escorting the ladies. That such a grown man should stand by and let a mere girl stop a duel is beyond my comprehension."

And still scolding, she let Lord Alistair lead her back out of the pasture and onto the road.

The shepherd grinned as he watched them go. It had been a rare morning's work and the funniest thing he had seen in years. My lord had kept him outside the gate with the sheep until things looked dangerous for that little minx what was up the tree. Gave him five shillings for his trouble, did my lord. A whole crown piece. And to get two golden boys from them weaklings, that was precious. Still laughing, he turned his sheep back into the road again to drive them on to their proper pasture.

"I have no stomach for breakfast, my lord," said Honey primly when they had reached the inn.

"I was not thinking of asking you to share it with me," said Lord Alistair plaintively. "I do like a quiet breakfast."

"Then have it," said Honey rudely. "Good-bye, my lord. We shall not meet again, I trust."

"I sincerely hope not," said Lord Alistair. "You are the most fatiguing female I have met this age."

She turned a hurt face up to his and he caught his breath. The green of her cloak brought out little emerald-green lights in her hazel eyes, and her hair burned like old gold in the morning sun.

"Good-bye," he said harshly, and turned and strode off into the inn.

Honey's carriage started the long descent into London. Fields and woods gave way to boxlike summer houses, standing behind their railed-off gardens, and miniature castles of villas. At last the villas and summer houses disappeared to be replaced by one continuous shop-dotted street. Large white signs urging travelers to try "Warren's" or "Day and Martin's Blacking" glared beside the road. The shops became better and more frequent, more ribbons and flowers and fewer periwinkle stalls. Now they rumbled onto the cobbles. Their destination was very near. Honey picked up the memory of Lord Alistair and tucked it away in the farthest corner of her mind, and began to wonder nervously what her aunt would think of her.

As they approached the West End, Jem stopped the coach from time to time to ask directions to Charles Street, which was where Lady Canon lived.

They bowled along Piccadilly with the Green Park on one side and splendid mansions on the other. The coach turned off Piccadilly, down Half Moon Street, along Queen Street, and around into Charles Street—and suddenly there they were with Abraham jumping down to run and knock on the door.

The door swung open and an enormous footman stood on the step. He was wearing a beetroot-colored coat with a cherry-colored waistcoat and breeches, the whole elaborately bedizened with gold lace.

Abraham gulped and pulled nervously at the

lapels of his new striped waistcoat to give him courage.

"Miss Honeyford is arrived," he said.

The footman nodded and stepped aside to be replaced by a very grand butler. Abraham and Peter rushed to carry Honey's meager luggage into the hall.

"This way, Miss Honeyford," said the butler. "I trust you have had a pleasant journey. My name is Beecham. I will apprise my lady of your coming."

He led the way up a flight of stairs to a saloon on the first floor, ushered Honey inside, and then retired, leaving her alone in the room.

Honey felt very nervous. On her arrival, she had only taken in a brief impression of a double-fronted town house with shallow marble steps leading up to a shiny black door with a fanlight.

The richness of her present surroundings intimidated her. A fire crackled under the marble mantel. Tall windows draped in long, thick, velvet curtains looked out to the buildings at the back of the house. Clocks ticked busily away. Backless sofas and elegant chairs which looked as if they were never meant to be sat on stood on their ornate legs on a pale-blue Chinese carpet.

There was a portrait of a lady with chestnut hair and hazel eyes over the fireplace. She was wearing a white dress with a blue sash and she was sitting at a davenport, writing a letter, while a French greyhound crouched at her feet. A lump rose to Honey's throat as she realized she was looking at a portrait of her mother.

She had known her aunt was a widow, but she had never guessed that she would turn out to live in such magnificent surroundings.

The door opened and Lady Canon came in.

She was a small, neat lady with snow-white hair under a frivolous cap. Her eyes were large and sparkling and very black. She wore a dove-colored velvet gown embroidered down the front with silk of the same color in a running foliage pattern of vine and olive leaves.

Her skin was good, and only faintly wrinkled under its coating of pearl powder, although she must have been in her late fifties.

She looked at Honey and then held out both her hands. "You are like Sophy," she said. "I feel as if I have my little sister back with me again."

Honey took Lady Canon's hands and bobbed an awkward curtsy.

"You must be exhausted," went on Lady Canon. "The reason you have not seen me for such a long time is because you live so very far away, and then I never leave Town if I can help it. We will have tea and you must tell me how Sir Edmund is and how you fared on your journey."

"Yes, my lady."

"No, no, you must call me Aunt Elizabeth. Now sit by me in front of the fire."

When tea was served, which Lady Canon insisted on making herself, she turned to Honey and said, "We are going to have an exhausting time with milliners and dressmakers and the like. It will be fun to see you *en grande tenue*. Is your back hurting you, my dear? You sit rather rigidly."

"It is my corset," said Honey. "I am afraid I am not used to such fashionable items, Aunt Elizabeth. It hampers my movements quite dreadfully. When I was climbing that tree, I thought . . ." Honey broke off in confusion.

"Climbing a *tree!* I must hear about *that*. No fashionable lady of your years wears a corset, Honoria. Very bad for the circulation of the blood. Tell me about the tree."

So Honey told about the duel, and about Lord Alistair, while Lady Canon listened intently, her black eyes sparkling. Without knowing quite how Lady Canon managed to draw it out of her, Honey found herself relating all her adventures on the road.

"I know Lord Alistair Stewart very well," said Lady Canon. "I cannot believe he behaved so badly."

"I am glad to hear you say so," said Honey

wryly. "I was under the impression that *mine* was the disgraceful behavior, not his."

"You have your youth and lack of sophistication as an excuse," said Lady Canon. "There are many hoydens such as yourself in society. Careless upbringing, my dear!" Honey gave a little gasp. She was secretly proud of her behavior and thought it showed independence of spirit, and yet here was Lady Canon dismissing it out of hand as typical conduct of any badly brought up girl! "But," went on Lady Canon, "for Lord Alistair to boast that he was rich, to abuse your clothes, to quiz you on marriage is past believing."

"In all fairness," said Honey, "he did try to be helpful."

"But so overbearing! Not at all his style. And to recommend that you frequent the Blue Stockings. That will never do."

"I think that was the only sensible thing he said," pointed out Honey.

"No, no, *no*. A young girl of radical mind is a dangerous commodity. You are to be a fine beauty and you will be married as soon as possible. Poor Sir Edmund is relying on you."

"I had hoped he would not mind were I to return unwed," said Honey in a small voice.

"No, of course he would not, for he loves you dearly. But he does need a man to help him manage the land, and it must have cost him more money that he can afford to send you to London. I tried to point out in my letter that I would gladly pay for all your clothes and amusements, but I know he will not hear of it. I sent him money before, you know, but he returned it with a most expensive gift. Every decently brought up young girl owes it to her parents to make as good a match as possible, and though Sir Edmund confessed to me that your upbringing had been very strange, there is a great deal of love and concern which must be repaid."

"But it seems so cold-blooded. How can I live with someone I do not love or respect?"

"Quite easily," said Lady Canon. "Bless the gentlemen! If it were not for their clubs and gambling, their prize fights and tedious parliamentary speeches, we ladies would be bored to death. Rely on it, my dear, one does not need to see much of the creatures, once one is wed."

"But children!"

"A necessary part of marriage. Unfortunately, I was not blessed with any. But there are wet nurses, nurses, governesses, and tutors. One does not need to see much of them, either. Marriage is a business transaction. If you want love, then you must wait until *after* you are married."

Honey looked wretched.

"Do not look so sad. You were not put on this earth to think only of yourself. You must pay your debt to your papa. Freedom! No such thing exists for an unmarried lady. Only after marriage may she do as she pleases."

"I will need to become like Amy Wetherall," wailed Honey.

"And a very good model too. She arrived shortly before you, and is already the reigning belle. A very pretty miss with charming ways."

"*She* is the cause of all this," said Honey passionately. "I was very happy as I was."

"I will forgive such an extreme show of emotion because you are overwrought owing to the fatigues of the journey," said Lady Canon severely, "but in future, never laugh or cry to excess, or show too much anger or passion. It is vulgar. Furthermore, it causes excessive wrinkles. But tell me about Miss Wetherall."

So Honey did, ending up by saying again that she did not want to be like Amy; she wanted to be on equal terms with men.

Lady Canon shook her head reprovingly. "You want a man to treat you as an equal, Honoria, but you must trap him first. Men must be manipulated, not ordered about. I must send a card to Lord Alistair. It would be disastrous if he broadcast your behavior.

"From now on, Honoria, you will be guided by me." The face was kind but the voice held a hint of steel. Honey looked about the pretty room as if seeing the prison bars closing in on her.

"Now, as to your servants," said Lady Canon. "Sir Edmund will be needing them, so they may rest this night and set out tomorrow."

Honey took a deep breath. She thought of Jem and Abraham and Peter, and how proud they were of their new liveries, and how they had talked endlessly of all the sights they would see in London.

"I am sorry, Aunt Elizabeth," she said firmly. "My father promised them they might have two weeks in Town. It is a visit that will last them a lifetime, and they have come a very long way."

To her dismay, Honey felt her eyes filling with tears.

Lady Canon turned her face away in embarrassment. It was quite shocking to see her dear sister's child reduced to crying over *servants*. But, better let her have her way, for the main thing was to get this wayward child brought strictly to heel as far as manners and dress were concerned.

"Very well," she said, "provided you promise faithfully to carry out your father's wishes, *and* my wishes, and behave as prettily as we *both* would desire."

Honey gulped, too tired and too beaten down

with all the conflicting emotions inside her to argue. She nodded.

"Good!" said Lady Canon with satisfaction. "You could easily take the crown from Miss Wetherall. Think on that, Honoria Honeyford. Think on that!"

Four

Lord Alistair, in answer to Lady Canon's summons, called on her at the end of the following week. Honey was confined to her bedchamber and surrounded by dressmaker's assistants, the terrifying dressmaker, Madame Vernée herself, and Lady Canon's dragon of a lady's maid, Clarisse Duval.

Lady Canon looked speculatively at Lord Alistair and thought it was a pity he was such a confirmed bachelor. He was wearing a corbeau-colored coat and the latest thing in scarlet waistcoats with kerseymere breeches and brown top boots.

He inclined his head gravely as she recounted Honey's view of the adventures on the road, but a look of faint hauteur crossed his face when she went on to say she hoped he would not talk about Honey's behavior to any member of the ton.

"I have been called many things, my lady,"

said Lord Alistair coldly, "but never, I think, a bore. I am not likely to prattle around the saloons about some fatiguing child."

"It is as I thought," said Lady Canon. "But you must see, I had to make sure."

Lord Alistair smiled at her sweetly and then looked vaguely about. "Miss Honeyford is gone from home, I see."

"No, she is abovestairs being fitted with new clothes. When I take the wrapping paper off her, she will take the town by storm. She is very beautiful."

"I fear Miss Honeyford's idea of taking the town by storm might not be the one you want, Lady Canon."

"Meaning she will behave shockingly? No, my lord, I find that a great deal can be done with the young and headstrong with firmness and kindness. So useless to humiliate them, don't you think? No one likes to be sneered at—even you, Lord Alistair."

"Oh, I have a hide like a rhinocerous," he said lazily. "Give Miss Honeyford my regards." He rose and made her a sweeping bow, and took his leave.

"Wonderful man," sighed Lady Canon, walking to the window and watching him walk off down Charles Street in the direction of Berkeley Square.

"Old *bitch!* thought Lord Charles venomously.

"As if I would dream of gossiping. That wretched girl would only cause me embarrassment. I must make a point of cutting her dead at the first opportunity, or goodness knows what fix she will land me in."

Honey did behave well. She felt she was in a foreign land, learning strange native customs in order to survive. Not only were there hours of fittings and pinnings, but hours of mock conversation with Lady Canon, who would take the part of the flirtatious man while Honey had to learn to parry compliments that were "overwarm" and gracefully accept the flowery ones.

And then, the day before her planned debut at the opera, Lady Canon announced that she was going out for most of that day to make calls.

She left Honey a pile of fashion plates to study and then took herself off in a cloud of lace and perfume.

Honey threw down the fashion plates as soon as Lady Canon was out of the door, and paced restlessly up and down. She decided to walk around to the mews to see how her servants had fared and to wish them Godspeed on their jouerney home on the following morning. Lady Canon would have expected Honey to summon the servants to the hall to make her farewells there, but Honey was itching to get out of the house.

Wearing her old brown silk and covering it with her sage-green cloak, she skipped down the stairs. She met her first setback in the hall. Beecham, the butler, loomed up out of the shadows.

"Are we going out, Miss Honeyford?" he said reprovingly, eyeing her hatless head and ungloved hands.

"Only around the mews, Beecham," said Honey. "I must say good-bye to my servants."

"Then I will send the second footman to fetch them here."

Honey ran past him to the door. "No, no, that will not be necessary," she said breathlessly. She opened the door and darted out into the street.

Beecham wondered whether to send a footman after her.

Then he decided to wait about fifteen minutes, and, if she had not returned by then, he would send John, the second footman, to fetch her back.

Honey whistled like a boy as she strolled around to the mews, the whistle dying on her lips as the full flavorsome smell of a London mews caught at her throat.

She found Jem, Abraham, and Peter just setting out to enjoy their last day.

"Where are you bound?" asked Honey wistfully.

"Over to the City," said Jem. "We wants to see the beasts at the Tower."

"Oh, take me with you," pleaded Honey, "and then I will leave you to enjoy the rest of the day."

" 'Twouldn't be fitting,' said Peter. "T'other servants say as how you're to be a fine lady now."

"And I am so weary, so *bored*," cried Honey. "Just let me come with you, just a little way. I have forgot what freedom is like."

"Can't see it would do any harm," said Abraham, shuffling his feet. He had a soft spot for Honey, and he hated to see his young mistress look so miserable.

"Yus," echoed Jem. "S'pose it won't do no harm. You run back, Miss Honoria, and ask her ladyship."

"She won't even know," said Honey triumphantly. "She's gone for the whole day."

The three brightened. "Then off we go," said Abraham.

"And we will pretend we are friends," said Honey. "Equals!"

"That's going too far," said Jem severely. "Them that doesn't know their place is flying in the face o' Providence."

"Jem, you are just as bad as Lady Canon."

"I know what's right," said Jem stubbornly, "so if you wants to come, you walk two paces ahead and we'll follow you up as we should."

As they were about to leave, one of Lady Canon's grooms strolled up. "Off again, are you?" he said jealously.

"Going to see the beasts at the Tower. Do you know of a good place we could get a bite to eat on the road?"

"The Cock at the head o' Fleet Street, opposite St. Dunstan's, is as good as any," said the groom. "Maybe I should get a place in the country, then I could go jauntterin' around for weeks like you lot."

"Come along," called Honey from the entrance to the mews.

They set out walking in the direction of the City, that great mercantile hub of London: the *real* London it had been before the Fashionables moved west. Along Oxford Street they went, peering into the shops, stopping to stare at the acrobats and tumblers performing at the side of the road.

They turned down the Haymarket and then through the Strand, stopping to see the wild animals at Exeter Change, which they all voted a poor shabby lot and hoped the ones at the Tower would be better. They darted across the busy road to look at the prints in Ackermann's Repository of the Fine Arts.

They stopped at The Cock in Fleet Street and had roast beef and salad and several bottles of canary wine, Honey paying out of the pin money her father had given her, and comforting her conscience with the thought that he would have behaved the same way in her shoes. Sir Edmund was more father than master to his servants.

Honey had had nothing stronger than tea to drink since her arrival at Lady Canon's, that lady having been so shocked over the description of the brandy drinking and, fearing Honey might be cursed with a Fatal Tendency, she had given her no alcoholic drink at all.

The wine went straight to Honey's head, engendering a light-headed, floating sensation.

As they went over Fleet Bridge, leading to Ludgate Hill, Honey quickly pulled out her scented handkerchief to block out the smell rising from the Fleet. Alexander Pope's lines swam through her tipsy head:

To where Fleet-ditch with disemboguing streams
Rolls the large tribute of dead dogs to Thames

Her servants had forgotten their rigid code of etiquette and were walking along beside her as they went up Ludgate Hill. A great crowd of people were hurrying in the same direction. Jem went over to one and asked where they were all going.

He came back, his eyes gleaming with excitement.

"There's a hanging at the Old Bailey," he said.

"A Lunnon hanging," said Peter. "But would it be right to take Miss?"

"Course it would," said Jem, pointing to carriages bearing several finely dressed ladies in the same direction.

The wine had now hit Honey with even more force and so she was not quite able to understand where they were going or what was happening, and so, before long, she found herself jammed in a swaying, shouting crowd outside the Old Bailey in Newgate.

Two men were being hanged for murdering a gentleman at the eleven-mile stone on Hounslow Heath, and a woman for stabbing her husband in the eye with a penknife.

Honey stared up at the gallows and felt sick. She wanted to escape, but she was pressed so tightly by the crowd that she could not move an inch.

The three condemned mounted the scaffold. Honey shivered, thinking of their plight, thinking of the dreadful night that had just been endured by these wretched people.

The bellman would have stood outside the condemned hole intoning:

THE ORIGINAL MISS HONEYFORD

All you that in the condemned hole do lie,
Prepare you, for tomorrow you shall die.
Watch all, and pray: the hour is drawing near
That you before the Almighty must appear.
Examine well yourselves, in time repent
That you may not to eternal flames be sent.
And when St. Sepulchre's in the morning tolls,
The Lord above have mercy on your souls.

They used to take the condemned to Tyburn where they were hanged just outside the gates of Hyde Park. Honey remembered her father telling her that it was quite common to see twenty-one people hanged at once.

"Boom!" went the great tenor bell of St. Sepulchre's. Honey groaned and closed her eyes and began to pray.

Then disaster struck. The crowd, anxious to hear if the prisoners were going to confess, surged forward. At the same time, a cart over-laden with people trying to get a better view, broke and collapsed. People falling from the vehicle were trampled to death. More people fell under the feet of the crowd as panic set in. The screams of the dying and wounded were dreadful. There were cries of, "Murder! Murder!"

The three prisoners kicked their lives out in the air above the screams and groans and curses of the crowd which surged forward and backward like the waves of some nightmarish sea.

Honey was separated from her servants. She felt she was being crushed to death. Her head swam. She was terrified of fainting, for she knew once she went down, she would never be allowed to rise again.

She thought of her father. She thought that all his care and concern were going to go unrewarded as his daughter met her end by being trampled to death at a public hanging.

"Nonsense!" said Lady Canon. "Gone to a *hanging!* I'll not believe it. It is too late in the day for a hanging in any case."

"This one was delayed, my lady," said Beecham, "on account of repairs to the scaffold. When Miss Honeyford did not return, I sent John around to the mews to find out what had happened. He learned that she had left with her servants but could not find out where they had gone. Then, after an hour, that groom, Perkins, volunteers the information that they've gone to see the beasts at the Tower, and that he had recommended The Cock in Fleet Street as an eating place. I did not like to trouble your ladyship with this until your return because Miss Honeyford was protected, and it seemed an innocent place to go.

"But just to make sure, I sent John after them, although they had a very good head start on him. He saw them ahead of him just as they were leaving Ludgate Hill to go to the hanging. He ran back here as fast as he could and I sent him on to Mrs. Osborne to call your ladyship home."

"He should have stayed with them," snapped Lady Canon. "He should have taken Miss Honeyford away."

"Begging your pardon, my lady, there's more. I had gone out on the step to send John on his way to tell you when Lord Alistair happened to walk past, and, seeing my evident agitation, he demanded to know what was amiss."

"Dear God, you never told him that Miss Honeyford had gone to a public hanging?"

"I am afraid I did, my lady. Lord Alistair said he would go in that direction and see what he could do."

"I do not see how he can possibly find one girl among thousands," said Lady Canon. "This is a wretched business. At least Lord Alistair will not talk. We must simply wait until she comes home. Do not look so worried, Beecham. I am not angry with you. You did everything you could."

And since the news of the terrible crowd deaths at the hanging had not yet filtered to the fashionable West End, Lady Canon decided to pass the time until Honey came home by preparing the lecture she was going to give that young miss when she eventually returned.

* * *

The screams of the crowd were deafening. Honey twisted her head, desperately seeking escape, and seeing only panic-stricken faces as everyone pushed and shoved and bit and clawed, trying to make their escape.

She knew she could not keep her senses for very much longer. She raised her eyes. Far above was the blue, blue sky.

There was another great surge as the people in front of Honey turned about and tried to push to the back. She stumbled backward against the buildings, feeling the black mass of the crowd beginning to press the life out of her.

And then she saw a rope dangling in front of her face.

She seized it tightly and screamed for help, her scream being lost among the screams and roars of the rabble.

Slowly Honey was pulled up above the crowd, although for several agonizing moments she thought she would never be free of the press around her. Her arms felt as if they were about to be pulled out of their sockets. A man jumped and struck at her but was knocked back by the stumbling and grabbing of the people about him. The blow sent Honey spinning out over a sea of upturned faces. Then she swung back toward the buildings and stuck her feet out to brace herself for the impact. The jolt when it came was severe, but she held on tightly to the rope and "walked" her way up the side of the building, praying her unseen rescuer would not let her drop.

"Hold the rope and let me get her," came a familiar voice. Lord Alistair's head and shoulders appeared out of the window. His strong arms seized her and pulled her in over the sill.

Honey fell in a heap on the floor. Lord Alistair eyed her with dislike.

When he had arrived at the scene of the hanging, he had been appalled at the chaos. There was no way of finding Honey among all these people. The screams of the dying and wounded were dreadful. The worst scenes were over at the corner of Green Arbor Lane, near Skinner Street. By vaulting over a wall which led to the back of the house, followed by his groom, Ben, he was able to bribe his way into the second floor of a house which overlooked the worst of the chaos. He hung out of the window and scanned the crowd below. Like a kind of mockery, the sun was shining brightly. Lord Alistair watched helplessly as a pieman dropped his tray, and, bending to retrieve the contents, was trampled to death. Several others went down with him, never to rise again.

He looked immediately below, attracted by

the screams from those who were being crushed against the buildings.

That was when he saw the sunlight glinting on a head of short chestnut curls.

"A rope!" he called over his shoulder to his groom. "Fetch a rope, Ben."

Ben was soon back with a stout rope. Honey was rescued. And now she was sitting on the floor at his feet and all he wanted to do was shake her until her teeth rattled.

"Do you know you were nearly killed?" he said furiously. "Don't you—"

He broke off as Honey struggled to her feet. "Give me the rope," she cried. "My servants! Oh, Jem and Abraham and Peter."

"Find them first," said Lord Alistair curtly, pointing to the window.

Honey leaned out, desperately searching the street below. "Jem," she cried. "He is there. He must have been quite close to me. Hurry! He is sore pressed, and Abraham and Peter are with him."

Lord Alistair and Ben lowered the rope carefully until it was dangling in front of Jem's face. Like Honey, he seized it, but, as he was being dragged clear above the crowd, Abraham grabbed his boots and held tightly.

Lord Alistair had removed his coat, and, in the middle of all her fear for the safety of her servants, Honey could not help noticing with surprise how his muscles bulged under the thin cambric of his shirt as he and Ben took the strain of two men dangling on the rope.

It had been an easy matter to lift a slip of a girl like Honey clear, but getting a heavy coachman with a sturdy groom hanging onto his legs over the windowsill seemed nigh impossible to Honey. But soon Lord Alistair and Ben dragged the coachman in and along the floor until Abraham catapulted through the window, still holding tightly onto Jem's legs.

"Now, Peter," said Honey, jumping up and down.

Lord Alistair gave her a sour look, but asked her to point Peter out, and to direct the rope. But the crowd about Peter were now anxious to get out by the same route, and they had to hoist up two strangers before they succeeded in netting Peter.

"Now," said Lord Alistair, "I think we should all get out of here as soon as possible."

There was a murmur of agreement, but Honey stood with her back to the window, her eyes flashing. "There are women and children down there," she said. "We should not forget them."

Lord Alistair looked at her wearily. He wanted to point out that his muscles were already cracking, that any woman who went to a public hanging should know to expect a riot, but there was something touchingly gallant about the small figure in the sage-green cloak, so he called to Ben and to Honey's servants to help him.

They rescued four women and five children before the crowd below suddenly began to make their escape as the mob on the outer fringes of Newgate began to disperse.

"Thank you," said Honey, impulsively stretching out a hand to Lord Alistair. "You were magnificent."

"I cannot return the compliment," said Lord Alistair icily. "I will return you to your aunt."

They had to walk as far as High Holborn before Lord Alistair could reclaim his carriage from the inn where he had left it.

"Make your way on foot, Ben," he said to his groom. "I would have a word with Miss Honeyford in private. As for the rest of you," he said, staring coldly at Honey's servants, "I am sure Lady Canon will have a few words to say to you."

Jem, Abraham, and Peter stood by miserably as Honey was helped up into Lord Alistair's high perch phaeton. They were in no doubt that Lady Canon would dismiss them from her brother-in-law's employ, and then write and give him the reason.

Lord Alistair started his lecture as soon as they were on their way along High Holborn. "Miss Honeyford," he said, "you are a most ungrateful girl. Your aunt has gone to considerable expense to furnish you with a wardrobe and to train you in the ways of society, and *this* is how you repay her."

"My father paid for my clothes," mumbled Honey.

"Don't interrupt," he snapped. "As I was saying . . ."

Honey sat and fumed. She had nearly been killed, and yet he had not offered one word of concern. He preached on and *on* about her lack of femininity, and yet he treated her worse than a man.

There was a great press of traffic when they reached Oxford Street. Lord Alistair let the reins drop and allowed his horses to edge their way forward.

Honey reflected that she would have enjoyed the novelty of sitting high above the crowd in this dashing open carriage at any other time and with any other companion.

Then she saw Amy Wetherall with her father and mother approaching in an open landau.

Lord Alistair stopped in mid-lecture and looked down at Honey in amazement. For she had started to laugh, a very charming laugh, and she was gazing up at him with a warm, flirtatious light in her eyes. He suddenly found it very amusing that he, of all people, should be playing the heavy father, and smiled back.

Amy Wetherall looked up and saw them—as Honey meant her to do—apparently on the best of terms. The traffic halted.

Amy remembered Honey because of her outrageously short hairstyle. "Miss Honeyford!" she called. "It is I!"

Honey looked down and raised her eyebrows with a pretty show of surprise before smiling and waving her hand in welcome.

Then both carriages moved on in their opposite directions.

"Who on earth was that ravishing creature?" asked Lord Alistair.

"Miss Amy Wetherall."

"Ah, the reigning belle. She is exquisite."

Honey folded her arms and glared straight ahead.

"Mama," Amy was saying plaintively, "do you not think my hair is unbecomingly long?"

"No, darling," said Mrs. Wetherall. "You are the most beautiful girl in London, and you do not need to alter your appearance."

But Amy bit her lip. Honey's hair, which had looked so *outré* in Kelidon, looked oddly modish in London. It *must* be modish to get a high stickler like Lord Alistair Stewart to smile at her that way. Lord Alistair had been pointed out to Amy a week before when that gentleman had been driving in the Park, and Amy had thought of him ever since.

Lord Alistair thankfully set Miss Honeyford down outside Lady Canon's home in Charles Street. His mind was full of the beautiful Miss Wetherall. There was a pearl! Miss Wetherall would not smoke cheroots, drink brandy, wave a pistol, or nearly get herself killed at a public hanging.

Honey was glad to get away from *him*, horrible, nagging man.

But the horrible nagging was not over, for Lady Canon was ready to deliver herself of her lecture. She ended up by saying she would take the liberty of dismissing Honey's servants and write and tell Sir Edmund why she had taken the liberty of doing so.

"Then you may dismiss me, my lady," said Honey quietly, "for they are part of my family. They are very loyal and obedient. I ordered them to take me with them, and they could not do else but obey. You *will not* dismiss them."

Lady Canon blinked a little at the quiet dignity in Honey's face.

Honey had not told her of the terrible crowd deaths at the hanging, or of her rescue by Lord Alistair. Let Lady Canon continue to think for as long as possible that she had merely gone to a vulgar spectacle.

"Well, well," said Lady Canon rather breathlessly, "*your* loyalty does you credit, and I will say no more on the matter. Your servants may return to the north as planned. But I expect *you*, dear Honoria, to give *me* the same loyalty. From now on you will behave impeccably. Do I have your promise?"

"Oh, yes," said Honey gratefully, prepared to swear anything so as to keep Lady Canon off the subject of Jem, Peter, and Abraham.

"Your debut is tomorrow night. It is all important," said Lady Canon. "Put off your cloak and we will continue your lessons. You have said farewell to your servants so you need not trouble about them again."

But although Honey really meant to reform, Lady Canon would have been very shocked if she could have seen her niece at dawn the next day, a niece who stood in the mews hugging her coachman and grooms, the tears running down her face as she said her final farewells.

Five

Honey had been looking forward to her first opera. It was Gluck's *Alceste*, to be sung in Italian. Although Lady Canon had told her the opera rivaled Almack's as a social event, nothing that she had said had prepared Honey for the reality of the spectacle.

It was certainly a place where the fashionable world went to be seen, so much so that some of the loungers strolled on the stage and danced about, which was rather disconcerting during one of the tragic scenes. Then when the lead singer was in the middle of the finest passage of a bravura song, several of the dilletantes in the boxes would scream out an accompaniment, shaking impassionedly the while, reminding Honey of nothing so much as two rival organ grinders competing on either side of the street.

The politer members of the audience would call out, "Bravo! Bravissimo!" even though they had been engaged in private conversation all the time the soprano had been performing, and then would turn to each other and say, "Vastly fine—what was it?"

So Honey contented herself with listening to as much of the performance as she could. But there was so much going on in the boxes that it was hard to concentrate on the stage.

And so it was that her wandering eye fell on Lord Alistair Stewart. He had just entered the Wetheralls' box and was bowing over Amy's dimpled little hand. Honey wrenched her eyes away from them and tried to concentrate again on the opera.

But she could not help wondering what would happen at the ball that was to be held after the performance in the opera house. Not that Lord Alistair would ask her to dance. Perhaps he would not even recognize her in her new finery.

Honey was wearing a light-green silk gown, embroidered with silver leaves. It had short sleeves drawn into quarters at the top of the shoulder and separated with broad silver chains. The bottoms of the sleeves and the hem were embroidered with silver leaves. The bosom of the gown was made entirely of lace and silver leaves. On her short curls she wore a dainty little tiara of gold and silver thread.

Beside her, resplendent in her favorite dovegray, sat Lady Canon. She was very proud of her niece, and noticed all the glances that were being cast in Honey's direction.

Honey was still shocked from her experience of the hanging. She was depressed because the opera did not manage to take her out of herself. If only all this was a bad dream, and she could wake up in her bed in Kelidon. She thought of her father's kindly face, and of how they would sit and talk of an evening, and her eyes glittered with tears.

But when they moved to the ballroom after the performance, she had no more time to think as a ring of courtiers started to form about her. Lady Canon introduced Mister This and Lord That and considered that Honey was behaving very well indeed.

The fact was that Honey, suffering as she was from delayed shock, mechanically remembered and followed all Lady Canon's instructions. She flirted with her fan and laughed her charming laugh. The film of tears across her large eyes made them look lustrous and hid the hurt and shock that might otherwise have shown through.

She danced with one and then another, trying not to wince, although her arms and shoulders ached abominably from the wrenching they had received the day before.

Somewhere, on the periphery of her vision, she was conscious of Lord Alistair dancing with

Amy. She wished he would leave the ball. He annoyed her by his very presence. It would have helped to have found society thought him a useless fop, but both men and women alike seemed to admire him.

And then Honey was asked to dance by the Earl of Channington. She dimly registered that he was tall and handsome and extremely well dressed—almost as well dressed as Lord Alistair. But then, no gentleman in London, it appeared, could compete with Lord Alistair, except, perhaps, that leader of fashion, Beau Brummell.

As Lord Channington swung her around in the figure of the country dance, she stifled an exclamation as the pain in her arms and shoulders became more intense.

He promptly stopped dancing, and, taking her hand in a strong clasp, led her from the floor, much to the irritation of the other members of the set.

"What is the matter, my lord?" asked Honey, afraid lest she had disgraced herself in some way.

"Miss Honeyford," he said, "my fairy princess, I was afraid you might break in my arms. You look so lost and fragile. Have you the headache?"

"No, my lord," said Honey. "I wrenched my arm yesterday and it still pains me."

"The guests are to go in to supper after this dance. Allow me to lead you to the supper room and we can be in advance of the party. I would protect you."

His voice was low and sincere. Honey looked at him properly for the first time. He had a square, tanned face and deep brown eyes which sparkled with an odd light but did not reveal what he was thinking. His mouth was long and thin. His burnished brown hair was a miracle of the hairdresser's art, and his evening coat was smoothed across his broad shoulders. Emerald buttons shone on his white waistcoat, emerald rings glittered on his fingers, and a large emerald shone from the snowy intricate folds of his cravat.

Honey nodded, and then asked cautiously, "Perhaps you should obtain permission from Lady Canon."

"Lady Canon has already given us permission," he said. "Look!"

Honey looked to where Lady Canon was nodding and smiling her approval.

He led her into the supper room, supporting her tenderly as if he feared she might break. "Wine for the lady," he called imperatively, while he drew out a chair for her and hovered solicitously about her until he was sure she was comfortably seated.

But Honey asked for lemonade instead, convinced that too much canary wine in Fleet Street had addled her brains so much that she had ended up at the hanging.

Immediately the solicitous earl was on his feet again. Lemonade. Immediately! Iced? It must be iced.

Honey began to feel cherished—a strange, warm, and comforting feeling. Lord Channington seemed to exude an atmosphere of protection, to throw a shield about the pair of them.

"Please try to eat something," he urged after Honey had been served with a cold collation and showed no signs of wanting to touch it.

"You are very kind, sir," said Honey. "I am not used to dining at such a late hour. I fear you will find me sadly countrified."

"Not I!" he cried. "I am the luckiest man here tonight. I have stolen a march on them all. They all wanted to take London's new beauty in to dine."

"The reigning beauty is Miss Wetherall."

"She was, until you snatched the crown from her. Your rare beauty makes every other lady here look sadly *earthy*."

Honey was not quite sure how to receive this compliment, so she smiled demurely and drank her lemonade.

Lady Canon had told her that high-flown compliments were the fashion, and so, much as she enjoyed this handsome man's flattery, she did not believe a word of it.

He asked her if she had enjoyed the opera, and Honey replied that she had, not wanting to seem provincial by criticizing the behavior of the audience.

"It was vastly fine," he said. "I saw a most odd comic opera t'other day. It was called *Whistle for It*. The songs were very elegant. But the opera itself was a very indifferent one. I could not conceive why the epithet 'comic' was given to it. Never was there a more complete misnomer. It was full of *terrific* situations, and ended with a prospect of a dozen or so persons being hanged. Miss Honeyford! You are become quite white."

"I think I *will* have a little wine," said Honey in a shaky voice.

The company began to enter the supper room to take their places at the long tables. Lord Alistair and Amy Wetherall sat down opposite Honey and Lord Channington. Honey cynically waited for Lord Channington to turn his attention to Amy, but his eyes remained fixed on her own face. Honey blushed slightly with pleasure, and Lord Channington was quick to tell her that the color enhanced her beauty.

Honey could not help stealing a glance at Lord Alistair. His sleepy blue eyes betrayed nothing more than his customary good humor.

It was hard to realize that this man had lectured her like a stern parent, that his powerful muscles had pulled her up from death.

Amy was wearing a demirobe of white Albany gauze over a soft, white, figured satin train petticoat. Her hair was worn in a plain band on the left side of the forehead, with a few loose waves on the right and two large corkscrew curls falling to the right shoulder. A rich Barcelona scarf trimmed with a narrow border of gold was hanging negligently over one arm. Her necklace and earrings were of cornelian.

Jealousy was adding a rather hard glaze to Miss Wetherall's beauty. She could not quite believe that the terrible Miss Honeyford, that gruff, eccentric little girl from Kelidon, had snatched the title from her.

Lord Alistair and Lord Channington were discussing the opera. Honey, Amy noticed, sat very still. She made no attempt to engage either gentleman's attention. This otherworldly pose of Miss Honeyford's would soon pall, thought Amy. Now, she herself was renowned as a conversationalist as well as a beauty.

She waited impatiently until there was a break in the gentlemen's conversation. "There are some vastly amusing Irish on-dits in circulation," said Amy.

"Since most of us here have at least a dash

of Irish in our ancestry, Miss Wetherall," said Lord Channington, "I fail to see why society should make a butt of that charming race."

"Oh, you are *funning*," trilled Amy. "Everyone knows the Irish are so *stoopid*. Do you not agree, Miss Honeyford?"

"I am sorry," said Honey, coming out of her reverie with a start. "What were you saying, Miss Wetherall?"

"I was saying I think Irish stories are very funny."

"Indeed?" said Honey vaguely.

Amy frowned a little at this lack of encouragement, but plunged ahead.

"There is this Irish surgeon who walks the hospitals who boasted lately that he had amputated many limbs, and that he received four pounds for each operation, which proved a slight compensation for the noise and uproar he was compelled to bear from the patients under his hands. 'Faith, Doctor,' said his friend, Mr. O'Brien, 'you carry on a *roaring* trade!' "

Everyone laughed dutifully, and, much emboldened at being the center of attention, Amy went on, "But the most priceless story I have heard in this age is about the Irish executioner. He had just received a very generous present from a malefactor he was about to execute, and wishing to thank him, he said, 'Ah, many thanks and *long life* to your honor,' and immediately pulled the bolt of the platform *and launched him into space!"*

Amy put her little hands over her face and rocked with laughter.

The effect on Honey was disastrous. She was transported back to the City, to the crowd, to the hanging. She could hear the screams of the dying. She swayed in her chair.

"Miss Honeyford!" cried Lord Channington. "I fear you really are unwell. Let me fetch Lady Canon."

"I think brandy is the answer," came Lord Alistair's cool, mocking voice.

A wave of anger drove away Honey's feeling of nervous sickness. "Thank you, my lord," she said coldly. "I have wine in my glass."

"Lord Alistair!" cried Amy. "What *can* you be thinking of? We delicate creatures do not drink brandy. You will be handing us cheroots next."

"I do not think Miss Honeyford is in a mood for jests tonight," said Lord Alistair. His blue eyes resting on Honey were now kind. He thought of all she had been through at the hanging, and realized for the first time that any other lady of his acquaintance would have had the vapors for at least a month. He decided the best thing he could do at that moment was to attract Amy's attention to himself.

He turned to her with a charming smile and complimented her on her gown.

"Do let me take you away from here, Miss Honeyford," urged Lord Channington. He lowered his voice. "Miss Wetherall is fatiguing company."

His attentive manner, his criticism of Amy, his handsome face and dark eyes were all balm to Honey's soul. She suddenly realized she *was* a success this evening. Only let Lord Alistair see how she could ensnare and entrap this earl.

She began to ask Lord Channington about his life in Town and whether he had estates in the country, and, ever mindful of her father's troubles, she went on to ask him if his land was in good heart.

"You must not spoil your looks with worrying over agricultural problems," said Lord Channington indulgently. "We men are here to handle that side of things. If I had my way, Miss Honeyford, you would not have to worry about anything, ever again."

A few days ago this pretty speech would have enraged Honey. But she was aware of Lord Alistair's blue eyes fixed cynically upon her, and she could not help contrasting Lord Channington's kindness and concern with what she considered Lord Alistair's brutal treatment of her at the hanging. Yes, and even at the duel! He was cold and unfeeling and she wished Amy the joy of him.

But his proximity continued to upset her and so Honey at last boldly suggested to Lord Channington that they continue their conversation in the ballroom.

He eagerly agreed, jumping up to draw her out of her chair and help her to her feet as if she were the most fragile piece of porcelain. Again, Honey felt that warm, secure, *loved* feeling, and left on his arm without giving Lord Alistair a backward glance.

Lord Alistair listened with half an ear to Amy's prattling. He was wondering when he could conveniently rid himself of Amy's boring company. It was always thus. Their brains never matched their beauty. He was also wondering whether to warn Lady Canon that her charge had fallen victim on the first night of her debut to the charms of one of society's most treacherous womanizers.

Channington, he reflected, was that most dangerous of Casanovas, one who always appeared more pursued than pursuing, one who managed to deflower young virgins without that fact ever coming generally to light, since the families of the girls did their best to hush things up. What made him most dangerous of all was that he always genuinely fancied himself in love with his latest victim.

And Miss Honeyford had looked very loveable, thought Lord Alistair ruefully. What a transformation! She did indeed look like the fairy princess that society had just dubbed her. But she had the insolence to actually dislike him! And after all he had done for her. Be damned to her! He was through with rescuing her. Let her find out about Channington for herself. Lady Canon would not know about Channington's womanizing. It was all part of one of those nasty little undercurrents one heard in the London clubs—never, of course, frequented by women.

He dragged his attention back to his fair companion.

Once more, she was trilling with laughter and rocking back and forth, peeping at him through her gloved fingers.

What a monumental bore!

Lord Channington sat at the side of the ballroom and chatted to Honey in a companionable way. He pointed out the notables to her and kept her amused with a slightly malicious fund of gossip.

Then, as the dancing was about to commence again, he said, "Let me suggest to Lady Canon that you go home. She must be delighted with your success this evening."

Honey opened her mouth to protest, but Lord Channington was already on his feet and was walking toward where Lady Canon sat with the dowagers.

She came back with him, all smiling concern. "Of course we may go, Honoria," she said. "Say your good-byes to Lord Channington."

Honey rose and swept Lord Channington a deep cursty. "I may call on you, my lady?" asked Lord Channington.

"Certainly," said Lady Canon. "We shall be at home in the afternoon tomorrow. Come, Honoria."

Somewhat to Honey's disappointment, Lady Canon did not offer any words of praise on the road home. But her aunt was very well content. She felt it was too soon to praise Honey. The girl had behaved magnificently, but praise might go to her head and make her reckless.

So Honey consoled herself with the reflection that there was a lot to be said for this business of being a young lady. She dreamily imagined Lord Channington back at Kelidon, taking all the cares of the estates from her father's shoulders. And beautiful gowns were not irksome to wear. The one she had on weighed very little and the tiara of silver and gold thread was lighter than any hat.

It was wonderful to be a success. Although she could not quite believe Lord Channington's flattery, she still had a warm glow from the memory of having had so many gentlemen waiting to dance with her.

It was the custom for the gentlemen to pay calls on the ladies they had danced with the night before, although some contented themselves by sending one of their servants around with a card, but she was sure Lord Channington would call in person.

She would dream of him that night.

But no sooner had she fallen asleep than she was locked in a dreadful argument with Lord Alistair. She wanted him to kiss her and he would not. She *begged* him to kiss her and he walked away with Amy on his arm, laughing over his shoulder. Honey awoke and lay there, *hating* Lord Alistair Stewart.

Lord Alistair awoke at the same time and lay looking at the rushlight patterns on the ceiling. He had had a very strange dream about Miss Honeyford in which he had been trying to catch hold of her on the ballroom floor to warn her about Channington, but she kept dancing away from him, always just beyond his reach.

She had looked very beautiful at the opera, he thought. Would any of the elegant assembly there be able to imagine a Miss Honeyford sitting in a repellent bonnet, drinking brandy and smoking cheroots? He smiled, remembering her spirit and fiery temper. Amy Wetherall would never dream of trying to stop a duel, nor would she dream of jauntering through London with her servants. And quite right, too! But Amy was a bore. He had heard her wit praised, and could only come to the conclusion that it was the old story—*anything* a beauty said, or the latest fashionable star said, was hailed as wit. Even the fame of Mr. Brummel's so-called wit was often due to that servile streak in society which made them fawn on the insolent and the impertinent.

Channington. What was the latest whispered on-dit about him? His target last Season had been the young heiress, Pamela Hudson. He had courted her assiduously, a courtship which her parents had encouraged. Then, at the end of the Season, the family had moved to Brighton, and Channington had followed. He had been seen quietly leaving an assembly with a blushing Miss Hudson on his arm. Her frantic mother had searched and searched, looking for her daughter all that night. Next day, it was all over town that Miss Hudson and Channington had eloped.

Two days had passed and then, lo and behold, Lord Channington was once more to be seen in society. Mr. and Mrs. Hudson put it about that dear Pamela was ill, had lost her memory, and had gone out wandering on the downs.

The Hudsons were very rich. In two months' time, Pamela was quietly wed to an impoverished younger son whose gambling debts were notorious. Channington swore his heart was broken and that Pamela had loved this other young man all along. But it was noted by the gossips that Miss Hudson quickly left any social gathering where Channington was present, looking pale and wretched.

There were other similar incidents, but, for some reason, Channington was always found to be innocent, or had proof that he was elsewhere when Miss So-and-So disappeared from home.

Channington was very rich. Some said he bought his way out of trouble. Lord Alistair believed he gained such an ascendency over his victims that, when he proved false, they would not betray him.

Lord Alistair turned restlessly and banged his pillow, which seemed to have been stuffed with bricks.

But Channington had never before, surely, pursued a young miss who carried a pistol, and knew how to use it. On the other hand, Miss Honeyford had changed and no longer was the tough hoyden of the London road. Lord Alistair gave his pillow another thump. She had behaved beautifully at the ball and had even managed to make Miss Wetherall appear silly and coarse.

He decided to get up and go for a ride in Hyde Park. A little fresh air and daylight were all that was needed to banish the haunting image of Honoria Honeyford.

"I cannot sleep," Honey was muttering as Lord Alistair was dressing to go out several streets away. "If I were at home, I could simply go for a ride. But I *can* go for a walk. No one will be awake, not even the servants. I can go to the Park and back before anyone is up." Her conscience gave a nasty jab. She had given her word to Lady Canon that she would behave like a young lady. But surely Lady Canon simply meant "seem to be behaving like a young lady." Honey gave her conscience a mental slap to make it lie down and jumped out of bed. She went into the adjoining dressing room, rubbing her eyes as she gazed at the rows upon rows of gowns and mantles, pelisses and spencers.

It would never do to appear in the streets of London finely dressed. Honey selected one of her old kerseymere gowns and covered it with her sage-green cloak.

There had been a shower of rain during the night and the streets smelled clean and sweet. Puffy little white clouds were chasing each other across a blue sky high above the chimneys.

Honey walked down Queen Street and along Curzon Street past Shepherd Market to Hyde Park.

Blackbirds sang among the leaves of the sycamore trees and the morning sun sparkled on the waters of the Serpentine. Honey began to relax and feel at peace with the world. The bad memory of her dream faded. The world was new and sparkling, and Lord Channington would call that very day. Could she love him? Honey thought she could, very easily.

The Park was deserted. There was not even one solitary rider on Rotten Row. For this moment, she had the Park all to herself.

She began to dance, singing as she went, under the trees. Lord Alistair came trotting along the Row on horseback, his horse's hooves muffled in the damp earth of the Row.

He reined in as he caught sight of the figure dancing among the trees. It simply *could not* be Honoria Honeyford. He had banished her from his mind. He had even begun to think more kindly of Amy Wetherall.

But the sun shone down on the chestnut curls, and only one lady in London possessed a cloak of that particular color and cut.

He dismounted, and, leading his horse by the reins, he walked toward her, making no sound on the thick grass.

She turned around sharply, sensing his presence.

"You," she said.

"Yes, come to take the glory out of the morning for you. Why the merry dance? Does the memory of Lord Channington lend your feet wings? Go carefully there, Miss Honeyford. Channington pursues 'em and woos 'em, but never, ever does he marry 'em."

"Just like yourself," said Honey coldly.

"No, not just like myself. To put it crudely, I leave their virginity intact."

Bright color flamed in Honey's face and she turned and began to walk stiffly away, like a young cat that has just lost a battle.

"Take heed, Miss Honeyford," he called after her, "or Channington will eat you for breakfast, gobble you up, and spit out the bones."

"You speak of yourself," Honey shouted back. "Never approach me again, Lord Alistair Stewart."

"Gladly," he said, swinging himself up into the saddle.

Honey ran lightly over the turf until she reached the gates of the Park. She half expected him to pursue her, but when she looked back, he had gone.

She was furious. How dare he spoil this wonderful morning by trying to besmirch Lord Channington's reputation! Lord Channington was *twice* the man he was. And out of all the people in London, why had fate brought Lord Alistair from his bed to plague her solitary walk in the Park?

Honey marched home, pulling the key which she had had the foresight to take with her from her pocket.

Everyone was still asleep as she gently unlocked the door and let herself into the house.

But when she got to her room, she found she was still boiling and seething over what Lord Alistair had said.

Well, she would *exorcise* him!

She sat down at the writing desk, sharpened a quill, dipped it in the ink well, and began to write.

"Lord Alistair Stewart," she wrote, "is abhorrant, abominable, acrimonious, angry, arrogant, austere, awkward, barbarous, bitter, blustering, boorish, brutal, bullying, capricious, captious, choleric, churlish, clamorous, cross, currish, detestable, disagreeable, disgusting, dismal, dreadful, dry, dull, envious, execrable, fierce, fretful, furious, grating, gross, growling, gruff, grumbling, hard-hearted, hasty, hateful, hectoring, horrid, illiberal, ill-natured, implacable, inattentive, incorrigible, inflexible, insolent, intractable, irascible, jaundiced, knavish, loathsome, malevolent, malicious, malignant, nauseating, nefarious, noisome, obstinate, obstreperous, odious, opinionated, oppressive, outrageous, overbearing, peevish, perplexing, pervicacious, perverse, quarrelsome, queer, raging, restless, rigid, rigorous, roaring, rough, rude, rugged, saucy, savage, severe, sharp, shocking, spiteful, splenetic, squeamish, stern, stubborn, stupid, sulky, sullen, surly, suspicious, tart, teasing, terrible, testy, tiresome, tormenting, touchy, treacherous, troublesome, turbulent, tyrannical, uncomfortable, ungovernable, unpleasant, unsuitable, uppish, vexatious, violent, waspish, wrangling, wrathful."

She sanded the paper and folded it neatly into a small square.

"There!" she said triumphantly. "*That's* what I think of *you*, my fine lord."

She undressed, fell into bed, and tumbled headlong into a dreamless sleep.

Six

Honey was not allowed to sleep late. Excited by all the floral tributes which had been arriving all morning, Lady Canon wanted to make sure Honey was looking as ravishing as possible when her callers arrived.

Honey was served with a light breakfast of dry toast and weak tea, Lady Canon wishing her to maintain her slight figure. Honey's stomach rumbled and grumbled rebelliously as she was eventually placed on a backless sofa in the center of the first floor saloon and told not to move a muscle.

Lady Canon was satisfied with her niece's appearance since her aim had been to make Honey appear even more beautiful in the eyes of society than she had done the night before.

Honey was wearing the latest calypso robe. Made of rich imperial muslin of a beautiful light yellow, it was finished at the extreme edge in a line of embossed silver and gold, worked in light, open flowers, ornamented down the front and around each side of the train, the center of which depicted stars worked in small pearls and fastened in the middle with a gold stud. This confection was worn over a rich white satin train petticoat, worked around the bottom with stars of pearls and dead gold to correspond with the dress. The sleeves were of white satin, tight across the shoulders and made to hang in small folds down the arm.

Over her head, "in graceful negligence" as Lady Canon's maid put it, was thrown a long drapery of white Parisian net, embroidered with a pheasant's eye pattern. She wore one of Lady Canon's finest diamond necklaces, and diamond earrings sparkled through the net that covered her hair—the idea that unmarried ladies should not wear precious jewels having been "exploded," as the fashion magazines put it. Anything that was out of fashion was "exploded."

Honey sat very still, waiting for the first of her callers. She was frightened to move, not only because Lady Canon had warned her not to, but for fear of disturbing the carefully arranged white drapery. She hoped fervently that Lady Canon would serve cakes with the wine. Honey intended to eat as many as possible. Her experience at the hanging had left her unusually biddable and she agreed to all Lady

Canon's instructions with uncharacteristic meekness.

The floral tributes from her admirers scented the saloon. A giant bunch of pink roses from Lord Channington held pride of place. Honey tried to pass the time by guessing which gentleman would be the first to call. Lord Alistair had not even asked her to dance, so he was not expected. And a good thing too, thought Honey fiercely.

But the last man she expected was the one who was first ushered through the door.

"Captain Peter Jocelyn," announced Beecham.

Honey would have jumped to her feet, but Lady Canon coughed a warning and so she contented herself by giving Captain Jocelyn a warm smile and holding out both her hands in welcome.

"Honey! I mean, Miss Honeyford," cried Captain Jocelyn. "I am delighted to meet you."

Honey introduced him to Lady Canon, who quickly quizzed the young captain to such good effect that within minutes she had decided he was no threat to Honey's possible romance with Lord Channington, and merely a young man from Honey's home town with no interest in her whatsoever who had merely called to pay his respects because Sir Edmund had asked him to do so.

Lady Canon then decided to check with Beecham to see if all the refreshments had been prepared. She murmured an apology and left the room.

Honey smiled tremulously at Captain Jocelyn and waited for him to comment on her new appearance.

"You do not look like yourself," was the first thing the captain said when they were alone. "You look like a guy with all that glitter and drapery."

"You are alone in your opinion," said Honey haughtily. She remembered her father saying that the young men of Kelidon would always see the Honey of the hunting field, no matter what she did.

"I say, don't stiffen up," pleaded Captain Jocelyn. "I called because Sir Edmund told me to tell you to write as soon as possible."

"I shall—today," said Honey. "So many things have been happening I have not had the time." She flushed guiltily as she remembered she had had time that very morning to write a list of insults about Lord Alistair.

"There was another reason, a selfish one," said Captain Jocelyn shyly. Honey smiled at him, liking again his honest face and clean-cut looks.

"It's Miss Wetherall."

Honey scowled dreadfully.

"What *about* Miss Wetherall?" she demanded crossly.

"You're such a good chap, I thought you might help me. I'm awfully in love with her and I need your help. I am frightened to call on her for fear of a rebuff, and I wondered where I might meet her by chance."

"I do not know," said Honey, controlling her temper. "I would think the best way to see her would be to go to the Park at the fashionable hour."

"That is what I thought. Perhaps I might be able to persuade you to come driving with me tomorrow afternoon?"

"Really, Captain Jocelyn," said Honey, trying on her grandest manner, "I have many social engagements and I doubt whether I will be at liberty to help you further your suit with Miss Wetherall."

He looked so crestfallen that Honey's kind heart was touched. For once, she recognized her own jealousy of Amy.

"On second thought," she said gently, "I am sure I could manage an hour in the Park. You must ask Lady Canon's permission."

"Of course I shall. You are the best of fellows."

At that moment Lady Canon came back into the room just as Lord Channington was announced. Captain Jocelyn waited impatiently

for the introductions to be over and then begged
permission to take Honey driving.

Lady Canon thought quickly. She did not
want to encourage Captain Jocelyn. On the
other hand, it would not do to make things too
easy for Lord Channington, and so she smiled
and gave her permission. Having got what he
came for, Captain Jocelyn took his leave.

Lord Channington thoughtfully watched him
go. He decided he must find some way of getting rid of this young captain before Honey's
affections became seriously engaged.

He turned to Honey and carefully began to
extract a list of her social engagements for the
next few days, although Honey had to appeal
to her aunt several times, not quite knowing
what Lady Canon had planned for her.

Lord Channington found she was to attend
Almack's the following night and begged for
the first waltz, but Lady Canon pointed out
that Honey had not yet been to Almack's
and therefore had not obtained permission from
the patronesses to dance the waltz.

Honey smiled and promised him the first
country dance instead. Soon her other admirers arrived. Lady Canon had put it about that
she meant to leave Honey her fortune in her
will, and so now Honey had everything necessary to secure her success. Lord Alistair's remarks still rankled, and so Honey played to

that unseen audience, that missing lord, as she flirted to a nicety, still managing nonetheless to eat as much as she could without Lady Canon's noticing.

And yet, Honey had been so sure Lord Alistair would call if only to give her another set down. But every time her thoughts strayed toward him, Lord Channington was at her elbow with another warming compliment. She found herself growing increasingly attracted to him and regretted her promise to go driving with Captain Jocelyn.

Lord Channington, like the expert seducer he was, had quite persuaded himself he was head over heels in love with Honey.

After he took his leave, he set out to track down Captain Jocelyn, and by dint of finding out that young man's lodgings, he set himself to watch his movements as carefully as a cat watches a mouse.

So it was, on the following day, two hours before Captain Jocelyn was to take Honey driving, that he found himself accosted by Lord Channington in a coffee house in St. James's.

Captain Jocelyn was flattered at the earl's attention and readily agreed to share a bottle of wine with him.

Since Lord Channington was obviously enamored of Honey, Captain Jocelyn felt it would be rude to point out that his own interest in

.s Honeyford was simply to further his own
..nds with respect to Miss Wetherall.

The captain was touched and amused to find
Honey being hailed as the toast of London society, but politely drank to Honey's eyes. Somehow the first bottle of wine was quickly followed by the second. And a third. The toasts
went on . . . to the King, to the regiment, confusion to the French, and so on, until the poor
captain's head began to reel.

Then, all at once, through a groggy fog, Captain Jocelyn heard Lord Channington reminding him of his appointment with Honey. He
leaped to his feet, muttering a hasty good-bye,
and staggered around to the livery stables to
collect the rented carriage he had bespoken
the day before.

Lord Channington smiled ruefully down at
the large puddle of wine at his feet. Most of
the glasses of wine he had raised in a toast and
then lowered under the table and spilled amid
the sawdust and oyster shells.

It would be fun to go to the Park and see the
drunken captain disgracing himself in Miss
Honeyford's eyes.

Captain Jocelyn was a full quarter of an
hour late arriving in Charles Street. In his
blurred and fogged mind, he had been expect-
ing the hoydenish Honey of Kelidon, and had
to blink several times before he recognized the

vision who was awaiting him—a vision who was studying him with some amusement.

Honey was wearing a carriage dress, a rich cardinal cloak of white satin stamped with small blue flowers and ornamented around the edge with an Egyptian border. Under it, she wore a simple white muslin gown enriched at the neck with Vandyke lace and at the bottom with three rows of richly-worked hemstitch. On her head, she wore a Danish bonnet of satin straw.

Captain Jocelyn bent over her hand, and continued to bend until Honey put her hand under his chin and pushed him up straight again.

"Are you well, captain?" demanded Lady Canon sharply. "You do not appear to be in plump currant."

Captain Jocelyn made one of those magnificent rallies that the very drunk can often achieve, and all at once looked sober and staid.

"Certainly, my lady," he said carefully. "May I assist you to the carriage, Miss Honeyford?"

He helped Honey up onto the high perch of a rather tired-looking phaeton, and then went around the other side and leaped up himself—only somehow he could not stop himself and shot on past Honey, took a nose-dive off the other side of the phaeton, and landed on the pavement.

Lady Canon fortunately had gone indoors and closed the door.

Honey was used to dealing with drunken men on the hunting field. She shouted to the open-mouthed groom who was standing by the horses' heads, "Help Captain Jocelyn into the passenger seat. I will drive."

She moved over and picked up the reins. "Don't know as I ought," said the groom, looking nervously at the four restless horses.

"Go to the captain and stand away from their heads," snapped Honey.

Captain Jocelyn was pushed up beside her, and she set off down the road, driving the team well up to their bits, and holding her whip at just the right angle.

"Mush she Miss Wetherall," muttered Captain Jocelyn sleepily.

"You will see her soon enough," said Honey, "but whether she will want to see you is another matter."

Honey bit her lip. She was torn between the desire to take the captain straight back to his lodgings and the longing to drive this four-in-hand in the Park. Perhaps Lord Alistair would be there, and would be able to see the lady he had damned as a fatiguing schoolgirl holding this mettlesome team in perfect control.

Vanity won. Honey swept in through the gates of Hyde Park, and, giving the team their heads, set off at a smart pace down the Row. She was so engrossed in her driving, so enjoying that old feeling of freedom and mastery, that she quite forgot about the captain and therefore was completely unaware he had fallen asleep. She did, however, notice that there was no sign of Miss Wetherall.

She had completed the round twice at a smart pace and was slowing her team to a comfortable trot when she came abreast of Lord Channington and slowed to a halt, her face flushed with triumph.

"Miss Honeyford," said Lord Channington, "your escort is in a disgraceful condition. My tiger will take my carriage and I will escort you home."

"No need for that," came a hatefully familiar, lazy voice. "Miss Honeyford drives better than any man."

Lord Alistair bowed and smiled and drove past.

Honey glared after him. She *hated* his calm assumption that she was equal to anything from nearly being killed at a hanging to driving this team.

She wanted to surrender the reins to Lord Channington and feel loved and cherished. But she could not disgrace Captain Jocelyn so.

"Captain Jocelyn is unwell," she said stiffly. "I am about to convey him to his lodgings."

"That would occasion a great deal of gossip, Miss Honeyford," said Lord Channington. "Allow me to take him. I know where he lives."

"Very well," said Honey, relieved. "Do make him understand I am not in the least put out and that he may call on me as soon as he feels better."

The drunken captain was heaved like a sack of coals from the rented phaeton into Lord Channington's carriage. Honey bowed, gathered up the reins, and drove off in style.

"Now my sottish friend," said Lord Channington, "let us make sure you do not trouble Miss Honeyford again."

At the captain's modest lodgings in Jermyn Street, Lord Channington asked his man for a pitcher of water and poured it full in the captain's face.

Captain Jocelyn woke with a shock from his drunken stupor with many Where-am-I's? and demands to know what had become of Honey.

With great and malicious exaggeration, Lord Channington told him of his behavior in the Park, ending up with, "So you see, my dear fellow, it won't do to go calling on her, for I fear she will never forgive you."

"But she must," said the still-drunk captain. "She promised to help me further my suit with Miss Wetherall."

"Do you mean to tell me," said Lord Channington, "that your sole interest in Miss Honeyford is to use her to get closer to Miss Wetherall?"

The captain tried to think of a more delicate way of putting it, but his fogged brain refused to work.

"Yes," he said baldly.

"The deuce," snarled Lord Channington. "What an infernal waste of good wine!"

He stalked from the room, leaving Captain Jocelyn staring after him in a bemused way.

Lady Canon was waiting for Honey, shocked to see her drive up to the door alone. A groom was sent to take the carriage and horses back to the livery stables. Lady Canon gave Honey a lecture on the folly of encouraging a young man who did not know how to hold his wine, and then went on again to lecture her about the visit to the hanging. For the gossip of the crowd deaths had reached Lady Canon at last.

"But there were several finely dressed ladies there," said Honey.

"They were probably cyprians or merchants' wives or low people like that. You must not disgrace yourself again by appearing in public on such friendly terms with your servants. If you must watch hangings, then a window can be hired—"

"Stop!" said Honey, appalled. "Do you know, Aunt Elizabeth, that I still have nightmares and horrors when I think of that barbaric spectacle? Never, ever again will I go to such an affair."

"Well, well, your feelings do you credit. Still, it is a mercy that such a high stickler as Lord Alistair Stewart did not see you there with your servants. Although he heard of it and went in search of you, it is as well he did not find you. There is nothing gives a gentleman more of a disgust of *anyone* as to see a member of the ton being overfamiliar with servants."

Honey was weary of her aunt's lectures and so did not tell her of her rescue by Lord Alistair. Drat the man! She did not even want to think of him. Almack's was tomorrow and she must be prepared to shine.

Lady Canon must have great social influence, thought Honey, to have acquired vouchers for Almack's for her. The patronesses ruled those famous assembly rooms with a rod of iron.

Many diplomatic arts, much finesse, and a host of intrigues were set in motion to get an invitation to Almack's. Very often people whose rank and fortune entitled them to an *entrée* anywhere were excluded by the cliquishness of the lady patronesses.

Honey gave herself an impatient shake. So little time in London and already she was fretting over a mere ball. She sat down at the writing desk and wrote her father a long and affectionate letter. Lady Canon had left to make a few calls and so the house was quiet.

Just as she finished the letter, a huge bouquet of flowers arrived from Captain Jocelyn accompanied by an abject letter of apology.

Honey sighed. She should never have given in to vanity and taken the captain to the Park. He might have come across Amy and then she, Honey, would have had that on her conscience.

She opened a book from her aunt's library entitled *Sacred Meditations* and settled down to read herself into a more serene frame of mind.

But the first paragraph that met her eye did little to soothe her. On the subject of women, the writer had this to say: "The happy timidity, the native gentleness, the maternal feelings, the muscular inferiority, and the parental infirmities of the female sex make them averse to the bold and fierce employments of uncultivated man. Their milder character is ever operating insensibly to soften his asperities and to infuse a softer spirit into his mind."

"Pah!" said Honey, picking up another book. This one promised to be more to her taste—*An Enquiry into the Best System of Female Education*, by the Reverend J. L. Chirol. Mr. Chirol based his argument on "an aggregation of incontrovertible facts collected in more than 500 schools," and then went on to say that even the best of them was good for nothing owing to the characters of the governesses at the English seminaries for young ladies.

"Some have been kept mistresses, cast off when the bloom of youth and beauty began to fade. Placed in a situation of reputed respectability, they soon make their fortune through the patronage of their former *protectors*, who obtain a right of admittance to the young ladies committed to their care and thus not infrequently indemnify themselves with these for the loss of the charms of their quondam mistresses."

And I cannot think of a more delicate way of putting it, as Lord Alistair would no doubt say, thought Honey, and threw the book away.

She finally settled down with *The Gentleman's Magazine*, which was more to her liking, and read an article where the writer considered women would make very good army officers indeed.

"Most women can dance and play with a fan, and they might be taught to swear," she read. "In fact, with a very little expense and trouble they might be rendered as formidable to our sex as many of the brave defenders of our garrisons, while they would be less dangerous to their own."

Honey's eyes began to close.

The heat from the fire was warm and the

ticking of the many clocks, soporific. She stretched lazily out on the sofa and went to sleep.

She was walking across a sunny meadow with Lord Alistair. His eyes were as blue as the sky above as he smiled down at her. He turned and took her in his arms. She watched his mouth descending toward her own and closed her eyes. The kiss was not what she expected. It was warm and rather wet. Furthermore, he had not shaved and his chin prickled. Honey opened her eyes in her dream and looked up into the dead brown eyes of Lord Channington.

She awoke with a start. Some horsehair was pressing through the upholstery of the sofa and prickling her cheek. She felt tired and cross and out of sorts. There must be some way she could banish Lord Alistair from her dreams.

Lady Canon was, at that moment, taking tea at the home of a certain Lady Maxwell and graciously accepting praise on the beauty of her niece from the other ladies present.

"I am very pleased to say," said Lady Canon, "that I have high hopes of Honoria's announcing her engagement very soon."

Immediately, she was pressed to reveal the name of the lucky man, all the other hopeful mamas wondering which eligible man they could knock off their list.

"Now, I cannot really tell you at this moment," laughed Lady Canon. "But a certain young earl is vastly *épris* in that direction."

All the mamas carefully ticked off Lord Channington in their minds. Then Honoria Honeyford's hopes and aspirations were forgotten as Lady Maxwell began to talk about an article she had read on the proper care of cooks. The article, she said, pointed out the necessity of frequent administration of physic to one's cook. The cook lived most of his life among unwholesome vapors exhaled by the coals, and the intense heat of the fire was pernicious to the lung and sight. The continual fumes arising from the stores, the vapors arising from the walls, and the amount of drink he had to pour down his parched throat, all combined to *encrust* the palate. "I did notice my Armand's ragouts were becoming too highly seasoned," said Lady Maxwell, "and so I called the physician on the spot. The wretched man prescribed two days' complete rest for my cook, which was quite impossible as I was giving a supper. I do not think one should *cosset* servants—even cooks!"

There were nods of agreement all around with the exception of a mousy, little girl called Miss Teesdale, who volunteered timidly that it might be more inexpensive in the long run to remodel the kitchen and make sure there was enough light and air. Everyone promptly pretended not to have heard Miss Teesdale, deafness being the weapon the aristocracy always uses to depress radical ideas.

Lady Canon at last rose to take her leave. To her surprise, Mrs. Hudson, an old friend of Lady Maxwell, accosted her in the hall and begged for a moment of her time. Lady Canon reluctantly agreed to drive around with her for a little. Mrs. Hudson was very rich, but did not go about much in society, and Lady Canon preferred to limit her friendships to those who were good ton. She was also worried that Honey might possibly have decided to get up to some mad escapade in her absence. But what Mrs. Hudson had to tell her in the leather-scented darkness of the carriage as it ambled around and around Berkeley Square alarmed Lady Canon into giving the unfashionable Mrs. Hudson her full attention.

The story of the seduction of Pamela and her subsequent enforced marriage to the younger son came out.

"But why did you simply not *force* Channington to marry her," said Lady Canon, appalled.

"Pamela had written him several very ... unwise ... letters," said Mrs. Hudson. "She promised him anything so long as she could spend some time with him. He threatened to have the letters published. He said he would make Pamela a laughingstock. He would claim that *he* had been seduced. We were terrified of the scandal. When he promised not to speak, not to talk about it, we were so relieved. Now, I feel I have let him go free to ruin some other young lady's life—some young lady like your niece."

"But Honoria has great independence of spirit. I cannot see her running slavishly after any man," said Lady Canon.

"Pamela was just such a girl until he broke her spirit. I beg you, Lady Canon, do everything in your power to keep your niece away from Channington. The man is a devil. At first he seems so very warm and kind and protective. There was another lady who fell victim to his charms. I tried to warn the girl's parents. They did listen to me, but when they ordered their daughter not to see Channington, she ran off with him."

"I will think of something," said Lady Canon firmly. "Thank you, Mrs. Hudson. I only wish I did not believe you."

Lady Canon summoned Honey to the saloon as soon as she arrived home.

"I have nothing arranged for this evening," she said. "I wish you to have as much rest as possible before the ball at Almack's tomorrow night. Channington seems very persistent. Do not encourage him."

"I find Lord Channington an extremely agreeable man," said Honey. "You are surely not going to *order* me to fall in love with someone else."

Honey's chin had a stubborn line and her eyes flashed.

Go carefully, thought Lady Canon. If I forbid her to see Channington, she might rebel.

"I have heard Channington is a womanizer," she said aloud.

"So have I," said Honey. "Lord Alistair was at great pains to point that fact out to me. Allow me to be my own judge of character, Aunt Elizabeth. Lord Channington's manner to me has been all that is correct."

Lady Canon decided she needed time to think and plan. She dismissed Honey, telling her to have an early night.

After Honey had left, she considered sending for Channington and warning him off, but such an experienced seducer might tell Honey, and then persuade her to go off with him.

What does one do to fight a seducer? thought Lady Canon, scowling horribly at the fire.

And then she had an idea.

Find another seducer, and the one would cancel out the other!

Seven

"You want me to *what?*"

Lord Alistair Stewart was shaken out of his usual urbanity.

"I want you to lure Honoria away from Channington and as quickly as possible so that she may fix her attention on someone suitable."

"I am relieved to hear you do not consider me suitable."

"You are a confirmed bachelor, Lord Alistair, for all your charming ways."

"Just *why* should I waste my time making a chit like Miss Honeyford fall in love with me—even supposing I could do so?"

"For the sake of the very dear friendship between your mama and myself," said Lady Canon firmly. "Also, you are a gentleman and I am asking you to do a chivalrous action."

"The simplest way is often best," pointed out Lord Alistair. "Why not warn Miss Honeyford that Channington is a womanizer?"

"I have tried, as you yourself have tried. I almost set her off in a contrary direction. She is very strong-willed. Come, Lord Alistair, a man of your charm and address should not need to waste much time on the matter. A week at the most. It should be a refreshing novelty for you. You have spent so long fending young ladies off, you should enjoy putting yourself out to attract one."

"I do not think Miss Honeyford likes me. In fact, I am persuaded she detests me."

"And what has that got to do with love?" said Lady Canon cynically. "You have not tried to court her. In fact, if her account of your behavior on the road be true, you went on more like a cross old uncle."

"I had reason, believe me."

"Then you now have reason to behave otherwise," said Lady Canon tartly.

Lord Alistair sighed and studied the polished toes of his boots. If he refused, Lady Canon would call on his mama, and his mama would call on him and would start to weep. Then, he found himself thinking of Miss Honeyford. A little time in her company would soon prove her to be as tedious as any other female.

Lady Canon studied him and wondered what on earth Honoria could see in Lord Channington when there was a man like Lord Alistair around. His face had a light golden tan which, together with his bright blue eyes and golden hair, made him look seductively handsome. He was wearing a dark blue morning coat with plated buttons. His toilinet waistcoat was striped with dark blue on pale blue and bound with silk binding. His long, well-muscled legs were shown to advantage in a pair of fitting, drab-colored kerseymere breeches which were fastened below the knee with gilt buttons. His brown Hussar boots winked in the firelight, reflecting the flames in their mirror-like gloss.

She had a sudden stab of jealousy and wished for a moment the roles were reversed and Honoria was the dowager and herself the young miss.

"I am waiting for your answer," she said.

"I am not yours to command, Lady Canon," said Lord Alistair mildly. "It is an outrageous request and I am trying to consider it at leisure."

Lord Alistair thought of Honey in Channington's arms. He found the picture exquisitely distasteful.

"I will see what I can do," he said.

"We are to go to Almack's tonight. It would be most gracious of you to escort Honoria."

"Miss Honeyford may not be very pleased to see me."

"As my niece, she has no choice in the matter," said Lady Canon, her black eyes snapping. Lord Alistair felt sorry for Honey.

"Besides," went on Lady Canon, "Honoria is the reigning belle. It will not be considered odd in the slightest when you start paying court to her. You were used to pay court to the reigning belles as a matter of fashion."

"That was in my salad days," he said ruefully. "I shall call for you at nine."

Honey, resplendent in a silver gauze ball gown embroidered with silver acorns, was blissfully unaware of her planned escort until the very last minute. She was too worried to think much about the ball because of the diamond circlet placed on her head by Lady Canon's maid, Clarisse. Honey was sure it had been bought specially, and cringed at the thought of the money that was being spent on her.

It only dawned on her as the hands of the clock approached nine that her aunt was unusually nervous.

"Are we still waiting for the carriage to be brought around, Aunt Elizabeth?" asked Honey, after that lady had looked at the clock for the umpteenth time.

"No, my love. Merely awaiting your escort."

"My escort!" Honey blushed becomingly.

"Then do not fear. Lord Channington did not

strike me as the sort of gentleman who would be unpunctual."

"Not Channington, my love. Stewart."

Honey did not have time to reply. The clock struck nine and Lord Alistair was ushered into the saloon.

Honey's lips folded in a mutinous line. Aunt Elizabeth should have warned her. She, Honoria Honeyford, did not want to make her debut at Almack's on the arm of a man who did nothing but find fault with her. She had told him to stay away from her, and he had shouted, "Gladly." But now he was smiling down at her as if they were the best of friends.

Anger lent a sparkle to her hazel eyes and color to her cheeks.

Lord Alistair looked formidably elegant in his black evening coat and knee breeches. Breeches were *de rigueur* at Almack's, the stern patronesses saying that only gentlemen with bandy legs or other defects in their extremities would be allowed to wear trousers.

Several of the young bloods had put in an appearance one night claiming to have bow legs and demanding that their legs should be examined to show they spoke the truth—all in the hope of embarrassing the patronesses.

It was they who were embarrassed when the patronesses took them at their word, inspected them, declared their limbs to be fit for breeches, and expelled them into the night.

Lord Alistair bowed and complimented Honey on her appearance. There was a tinge of mockery in his drawling voice and Lady Canon flashed him a warning look.

Honey's first impression of Almack's was that it was a very depressing place. The floor was not very good and the dancing area was roped off like a cattle pen. There was nothing stronger to drink than orgeat or lemonade, and the sandwiches were already curling at the edges in a tired way as if this were not their first ball.

But then, Almack's had never wasted much money on appearances since it was first opened by that shrewd Scotchman, McCall. By keeping the price of admission high, and by pandering to the Exclusives, he soon had it well enough furnished by the most glittering members of society.

The great George Brummell was already there, standing in a *dégagé* attitude with his fingers in his waistcoat pocket, talking earnestly to the Duchess of Rutland. The exercise of Brummell's power lay in his making rules, setting tastes, establishing standards for the management of those things that the superior world considered superior to all else. Once, when a duchess offended him, Brummell said, "She shall suffer for it. I'll chase her from society; she shall not be another fortnight in existence."

George Brummell could not possibly have risen to such eminence in any other period in history. Society was beginning to relax now that the fears engendered by the American War of Independence and the French Revolution were over. Once more they felt secure and they needed a ringmaster to direct their play in such a way that the crude lower classes were kept out of it.

The lady patronesses were all out in force: Lady Castlereagh, Lady Jersey, Lady Cowper, Lady Sefton, Mrs. Drummond Burrell, Princess Esterhazy, and Countess Lieven.

Unlike most dowagers, Lady Canon advised Honey to steer clear of Mr. Brummell and not to put herself in the way of talking to the patronesses unless absolutely necessary. Reputations had been ruined by young misses coming across one of the despots of the ton in a dyspeptic mood. "You can never tell when someone's spleen is going to be out of order," as Lady Canon put it.

At first, Lady Canon thought Lord Alistair had forgotten his promise. He was nowhere to be seen among the crowd of men surrounding Honey, but Channington most certainly was.

But Honey had promised the waltz to Lord Alistair, since it seemed Lord Alistair had the power to extract permission from the patronesses to lead her in that shocking dance, and, furthermore, Honey had become worldly-wise enough not to ruin her reputation by giving Lord Alistair a setdown in the middle of Almack's. That could wait until later.

She danced the first country dance with Lord Channington, and there was not much opportunity for conversation during the dance. But as the custom was to promenade with your partner afterward, Lord Channington made the most of the opportunity, shaking his head over the news that Honey had been escorted to the ball by Lord Alistair, and warning her delicately that Lord Alistair had a heart as hard as flint.

He then told Honey several shocking stories about the capricious cruelty of the patronesses, cleverly implying that, of course, no one would dare to harm her as long as he was at her side, and so conjured up that charming, warm feeling of security which seemed to draw the two of them closer together.

So expert was he at *binding* her to him that she felt quite cold and nervous when Lord Alistair took her away to lead her into the waltz.

Honey had danced the waltz before and it was no novelty to have a man's hand on her waist. But there was something so overwhelmingly *physical* about the nearness of Lord Alistair's body, and the small of her back seemed to burn and throb under the light pressure of his gloved hand. It was like those dreadful, shocking dreams. She stared at his top waistcoat button and stumbled over his feet.

"Miss Wetherall is looking at us," came his mocking voice from somewhere above her head. "I do wish you would look up, Miss Honeyford. Your diamond circlet is very pretty, but the light from it is blinding my eyes."

Honey looked up defiantly and found her gaze trapped and held by his own. He saw the mixture of innocence and wariness in those wide hazel eyes and felt a strange emotion which he did not recognize because he had never before felt tender or protective about any woman he had held in his arms.

"You are very beautiful tonight," he said without a trace of mockery. There was something in his eyes that made Honey's spirits lift and lift, until it seemed there was only the two of them moving through a brightly colored world.

Captain Jocelyn had secured the waltz with Amy Wetherall, a young lady of whom the patronesses highly approved. He felt he would be transported to seventh heaven if only Amy would look at him just once and stop glaring at Honey and Lord Alistair.

He envied Lord Alistair, who seemed to have the capacity to bewitch women. Only look at the way Honey floated in his arms, a Honey so transformed that Captain Jocelyn saw her for the first time as the new reigning beauty of London society and not as the muddy, swearing Honey of the hunting field. He felt a pang of regret. Amy would never, ever look at him like that. Perhaps he should have courted Honey, but anyone could see she was lost to any man other than Lord Alistair.

The patronesses languidly waved their fans and whispered that Lady Canon must be addled in her upper chambers to allow her niece to waste time with Lord Alistair Stewart.

The dance came to an end and Honey looked dizzily up at Lord Alistair. He smiled down at her in a caressing way and said, "Let us go and find some horrible refreshment. The cakes they have at Almack's are reputed to have seen more balls than I. I feel one should try to eat one of the things if only to send it at last to an honorable grave."

"I would like some lemonade," said Honey dreamily. "I am very thirsty."

He led her to a sofa in the corner of the room and sat down next to her. "Aren't you going to fetch anything?" asked Honey.

"Not I. The minute I leave your side you will be snatched away from me. I will find someone else to do the work. Ah, Channington. The very man. Miss Honey is parched and craves a glass of lemonade."

"Your servant." Lord Channington bowed to Honey and darted away to fetch the lemonade.

"You see how easy it is?" said Lord Alistair. "Now I do not have to exert myself in the least."

"But Lord Channington will expect to join us."

Lord Alistair smiled at her sweetly but did not reply.

Lord Channington came back, nearly spilling the lemonade from the glass in his haste.

There was only room on the sofa for Honey and Lord Alistair, so Lord Channington had to stand in front of them.

"May I beg you for the next dance?" asked Lord Channington.

"Miss Honeyford is fatigued," said Lord Alistair, "and, besides, she cannot dance while holding a glass of lemonade."

Honey opened her mouth to say she would like to dance with Lord Channington very much, but Lord Alistair went on, "Furthermore, Channington, there's Brummell signaling to you."

Lord Channington twisted about. "I cannot see George," he said.

"Course you can't," said Lord Alistair languidly. "He is over there, behind that pillar, under the musicians' gallery."

Lord Channington bowed and moved off. Several other gentlemen came up to ask Honey to dance, but Lord Alistair said, "You must all go away this instant. Miss Honeyford has promised to sit quietly with me and drink her lemonade. You cannot possibly want to offend me by taking her away."

Honey turned to him after her gallants had left and said in a hard little voice, "You do not own me, my lord."

"I have a prior claim on you," he said. "I saved your life. You are bound to me by ties stronger than iron."

"I am bound to no one."

"I would keep you by me, Miss Honeyford."

"Why?" said Honey sharply.

"What a disconcerting female you are. When a gentleman pays you a compliment, you do not glare at him like a scalded kitten and demand, 'Why.' "

"I told you to keep away from me," said Honey, "and you shouted, 'Gladly.' "

"My dear Miss Honeyford, I can no more keep away from you than the moth from the flame," he mocked. "I was seduced a long time ago by your fiery temper, your repellent hat, and the adorable way you glare at me. Bother! It seems we set the fashion. Miss Wetherall and her gallant have just sat down on the other side of the pillar. The young man is dazzled, but the fair Amy will begin to talk very loudly and clearly for our benefit."

"For *your* benefit," said Honey.

"I am persuaded Miss Amy would not give a rap for me were she not so jealous of you."

"Jealous of *me?*" Honey felt a warm glow.

"Oh, yes, very much so. Ah, there goes the laughter. Now comes the joke."

"So much do the Irish consider their own eggs, Captain Jocelyn," came Amy's voice, "the superior in sweetness and flavor to those in England, that some Irishmen will not allow that an English hen can lay a *fresh egg.*"

A burst of hearty laughter from the captain greeted this joke. Then he said, "Miss Wetherall, your eyes are like stars . . ."

"The Irish are *so* funny," went on Amy in an even louder voice. " 'I am very bad, Pat,' said one poor fellow, rubbing his head, to another. 'Ah! Then, may God keep you so, for fear you should be worse,' was the reply."

"Indeed! Jolly good. Hah, hah," said the captain with more duty than mirth.

"Dear me," murmured Lord Alistair. "We must move, or she will not stop, and here comes Colonel O'Connell, who is noted for his choler. One of Miss Wetherall's jokes would give the poor man an apoplexy."

He rose to his feet and held out his arm.

"No, Lord Alistair," said Honey firmly. "You are paying me too much attention and it is not the thing. You are driving away all my other suitors." She got up. "I do not know what possessed my aunt to encourage you in this way."

He turned and faced her, standing very close to her. "Promise me the next waltz," he said.

She took his arm and began to walk to the edge of the dance floor with him. "Promise," he whispered, "or I shall take you in my arms right in front of Sally Jersey and kiss you until you scream."

"You would not dare."

"Do not put it to the test."

She looked up into his eyes, seeing all the tenderness and amusement there, and something else she could not recognize. She weakly found herself promising him the next waltz.

Lord Channington, leading her into the next country dance, found her strangely abstracted. When he promenaded with her after the dance, he had to repeat things twice. Honey was floating about in a daze.

"Perhaps it will serve my ends," thought Lord Channington cynically. "When she finds out Stewart does not mean to marry her, she will come rushing to my arms."

Perhaps the only guest at the ball who was not firmly convinced that Honey and Lord Alistair were falling in love was Lady Canon. Having never been in love herself, she was incapable of recognizing that emotion in oth-

ers. Sophy, Honey's mother, had fallen deeply
in love with Sir Edmund. Lady Canon had
been distressed by her beautiful young sister's
marriage to a country gentleman of no particular fortune, and felt she herself had made up
for this lapse by carefully allying herself with
the wealthy Sir Angus Canon, a man consider-
ably older than herself who had had the good
taste to take himself off to his Maker after
only five years of marriage, and to leave his
widow all his worldly goods. Lady Canon often
thought of her husband with deep affection.

As a young widow, she had enjoyed various
discreet flirtations without ever once letting
her head rule her heart. It was a pity Honey
was so like her mother, but, with good luck
and good guidance, the girl should be persuaded
to settle for a suitable match.

Even if Lord Alistair had been interested in
marriage, his rank was too high above Honey's
to take the matter seriously.

Lord Alistair was holding Honey in his arms
once more as they circled in the steps of the
waltz. She appeared more relaxed in his company and even raised her head and laughed at
something he was saying.

It would do her standing in society no harm,
reflected the worldly-wise Lady Canon, when
it came about that Lord Alistair was not interested in her. Any girl he had favored with his

attention automatically became the rage. Brummell might dictate who was *in* and who was *out*, but Lord Alistair's interest decided which was the most attractive girl.

He must have a mistress somewhere, reflected Lady Canon. A man like Lord Alistair would certainly not lead a celibate life. Again, she felt that little pang of jealousy but did not recognize it for what it was, since she had hardly ever been jealous of any woman in her life.

"Why did you go to the Park so early?" Lord Alistair was asking Honey.

"I felt I had to get some fresh air," said Honey. "I could not sleep. And please do not lecture me on the folly of going out without a footman. I am now reformed. I am become civilized, you see."

"No more pistols, hangings, brandy, or cheroots?"

"No more hangings. How can people wish to see such a spectacle?"

"Thousands go every day. A friend once told me he got an exhilarating feeling from seeing other people die and knowing he himself was still alive."

Honey shuddered. "Perhaps that explains the behavior of my servants. They are all decent, God-fearing men."

"Think of something else," urged Lord Alistair. "What do you think of the famous Almack's?"

"Very fine," said Honey cautiously, "and not so grand or terrifying as I had imagined."

"Very terrifying for most, I can assure you. The fear of being excluded haunts them all."

Honey sighed. "It seems so petty. If I were a man, I should not care for such amusements. I would stay in the country and never come to London."

"You crave the simple life?"

"Do not mock me. A home where one can be free and happy is a wonderful place."

"You sound wistful, as if that home is something lost to you. You will soon have a home of your own, and children."

"But not love," said Honey, and then cursed her unguarded tongue.

"Why not love?" he asked softly.

"Oh, Aunt Elizabeth says that one may have a love affair *after* one is married, but marriage itself should be a business contract."

He looked down at her glowing face, at her eyes which were large and shadowed, and had a sudden impulse to wring Lady Canon's neck.

"A great many of my friends," he said gently, "were very eligible men and they married for love. They adore their wives and children. A suitable marriage need not be loveless."

"I do not think either you or Aunt Elizabeth

know the first thing about love," said Honey candidly.

"And you do, my child?"

"I have an awareness of it," said Honey. "My lord! You are holding me too close."

"True," he said lightly. "You make me forget myself, Miss Honeyford."

He held her the regulation twelve inches away from him and they ended the dance in silence.

Since he had danced with her twice, Honey did not expect to see him again that evening and was surprised when three in the morning arrived and Lady Canon announced that Lord Alistair was ready to take them home.

Although Lord Alistair and Lady Canon carried most of the conversation on the road home, Honey was intensely aware of him. She longed for him to take his leave so that she could be comfortable again, and, at the same time, she wanted him to stay so that he might look at her again with that special caressing look in his eyes.

Lady Canon invited him in to share the tea tray, and, after a little hesitation, he accepted. But he felt Lady Canon was going too far when she found an excuse to leave the room as soon as tea was served.

Lord Alistair sat down next to Honey on a sofa in front of the fire. The flames sent red sparks dancing from the circlet of diamonds in her hair.

"The gentleman who Miss Wetherall was regaling with Irish bulls . . . do you know him, Miss Honeyford?"

"Yes, he is Captain Jocelyn from Kelidon. He is home on leave. We went hunting together," said Honey dreamily, remembering nostalgically the freedom of the old days. It was hard to remember that "the old days" were only a few weeks ago, when she had last gone hunting.

"I think you have a *tendre* for him," said Lord Alistair.

Honey colored. "Not I. But he is the kind of man who would make me a suitable husband, I think."

"And not someone such as I?"

"Oh, my lord, all the world knows you do not wish to marry."

"Strange. It may be because everyone has been pointing out to me of late what a confirmed old bachelor I am that I have a strong inclination to prove them wrong."

"I do not think you should even contemplate the idea," said Honey, pouring tea. "You would only bully your poor wife to death."

"Not if I loved her."

Honey's hand shook and she spilled tea into his saucer.

"Do not worry," he said. "I do not really want tea, nor do I want to be compromised by Lady Canon."

"Aunt *has* left the door open," said Honey, "so you are not compromised. Only ladies are compromised."

"Gentlemen can have their hearts stolen, however, and I find your presence too disturbing, Miss Honeyford. The temptation to kiss you is almost irresistible."

"It is as well I know your wit, my lord. You are funning."

"Perhaps. In any case, give Lady Canon my regards and tell her the folly of her ways. I am going to my club."

He rose to his feet and Honey rose as well.

He took her hand and raised it to his lips. He had meant to deposit a light kiss on her gloved hand, but the little hand in his trembled and her eyes were large and frightened.

The strong current of emotion emanating from each of them held them both shocked. His grasp on her hand tightened and he pulled her toward him.

Her lips parted in a tremulous smile under the intensity of his gaze. Slowly, he drew her into his arms and held her against his chest, wondering whether it was her body that was burning and throbbing with such emotion or his own.

The watch called the hour outside the window, the fire crackled in the hearth, and the clocks ticked, while Lord Alistair and Honey stood very still, deaf and blind to anything outside the pair of them.

"You are trembling," he said huskily, his voice sounding strange in his ears.

"I think you had better let me go," said Honey in a small voice.

He released her immediately and thought he had never before in all his life felt so cold and bereft.

"Tomorrow," he said. "Where will you be tomorrow?"

"I do not know," said Honey.

"Here I am," cried Lady Canon brightly, tripping into the room.

"I am on the point of taking my leave," said Lord Alistair.

"So soon? I am sorry I left you so long, but my Clarisse is having hysterics over a trifle. The French are so incalculable, don't you think?"

"I must go," said Lord Alistair. "I shall see you tomorrow, Miss Honeyford."

"Ah, yes," said Lady Canon, "we are to go to Maxwell's *fête champêtre*."

"Then I will escort you," said Lord Alistair, his eyes, hooded and enigmatic, fixed on Honey.

"Of course," smiled Lady Canon, pleased

that Lord Alistair was taking his duties so seriously. "We will expect you at noon. Honoria! You have forgot to make your curtsy to Lord Alistair."

Honey went to bed that night in Lord Alistair's arms. As soon as she fell asleep, he was there, holding her close, straining her to him. She kissed him back with rising passion, begging for more and more intimacies, until he suddenly said, "Damn it to hell!" and got up and walked away, leaving her suddenly awake with the tears running down her cheeks.

"Damn it to hell!" muttered Lord Alistair savagely as he left Watier's and walked along Piccadilly to clear his head. He could not stop thinking of her. He wanted her. He wanted her so badly he could scream.

He must tell Lady Canon he could not see the girl again. "Why not?" mocked a voice in his head. "You could marry her and have her to yourself for the rest of your life."

"She would bore me," he said aloud, much to the amusement of a passing party of bloods.

"Then let someone else have her," sneered the voice. "Let Channington take her in his arms and . . ."

He walked faster, as if to leave the voice behind. He would see her, just one more time, and then he would tell Lady Canon he had done as much as any man could be expected to do.

*   *   *

Lord Alistair arrived promptly at noon, surprising Lady Canon by rolling up in a closed carriage. He said that his valet's left leg forecast rain and was more reliable on the subject of the weather than any farmer's almanac.

Lady Canon looked pointedly at the blue cloudless sky and then said she did not believe in encouraging servants to be dramatic.

Lord Alistair's coachman was driving and two tall footmen stood on the backstrap. He took his place inside the carriage facing Lady Canon and Honey—who would not look at him.

The fête was to be held in the Surrey fields. Honey was wearing one of the new gypsy bonnets and a simple white muslin gown embroidered with a dead gold key pattern around the hem. A heavy cashmire shawl was draped around her shoulders.

Lord Alistair thought she looked very pretty and said so, and Lady Canon prodded Honey in the ankle with her parasol when her niece made no response to the compliment.

Honey was terrified to find her dreams were coming to life. Her whole body seemed to ache and yearn in the presence of Lord Alistair. Her knees trembled and she pressed them together, praying for this agony of proximity to be at an end.

As if sensing her discomfort, Lord Alistair

moved along the opposite seat until he was facing Lady Canon.

Lady Canon began to chat about various people Honey did not know, and soon, as Lord Alistair appeared to become unaware of her, she began to relax and enjoy the sunny view from the carriage window.

When they arrived, Lady Canon was appalled to find that there were to be "no servants" present. They were all to sit on the grass and cook their own meals over open fires—that is, after an army of servants had lit the fires and arranged the food to be cooked in trays beside each party, before retiring a discreet distance.

Lord Alistair spread a carriage rug for Honey beside one of the fires and sat down next to her. A party of young ladies, including Mrs. Osborne, whom Honey recognized from the inn at Barnet, promptly joined them, teasing Lord Alistair and begging him show them what to do.

He replied to their sallies with great good humor, and Honey felt like sulking. She longed to be able to say something witty and bright to regain his attention. What a dreadful day it was turning out to be! Even Lord Channington was not around to raise her morale.

She could not join in the pretense of not knowing what to do, since the servants had left sausages and carefully sharpened sticks beside each fire so that the lords and ladies could play at being gypsies with very little effort.

Honey speared a sausage on a stick and held it over the fire. Lord Alistair handed around champagne and then said, "Only follow Miss Honeyford's example, ladies. *She* is never at a loss to know what to do, which is why I dance attendance on her." Honey received several sour looks, and one by one the ladies began to drift away to find gentlemen who would pay them more attention.

Lord Alistair took the stick from her and smiled down at her. "Let me look after you this day, my independent friend." Honey smiled back at him, dizzy with gladness because he had called her "friend."

All at once the day took on a glitter and sparkle like the champagne in their glasses. Lord Alistair did a fair imitation of Amy and invented terrible Irish jokes until Honey was helpless with laughter. They both agreed that food cooked in the open air tasted quite dreadful, drank more champagne, and laughed at the slightest thing.

The weather changed so suddenly and violently that it took the whole party by surprise. One minute, it seemed, the smoke from the bonfires was rising up to a clear blue sky, and the next, an angry wind was whipping ashes over the dresses of the ladies as the sky above grew blacker and blacker.

Lord Alistair got to his feet and pulled Honey up after him.

"Quick! To the carriage," he said, seizing Honey's hand and starting to run.

Still laughing, she ran after him, trying to keep up with his long strides. They reached the carriage just as the heavens opened and the rain poured down.

"My valet's leg is never wrong," said Lord Alistair, helping Honey inside. "I trust you did not get too wet?"

"Not very," said Honey, taking off her hat and shaking raindrops from it. "Where is Lady Canon?"

He rubbed the glass of the window with his sleeve and looked out.

"Dear me," he said. "What a wickedly bad chaperone that lady is. She is just climbing into Mrs. Osborne's carriage for shelter."

"Oh," said Honey, suddenly shy.

He sat next to her and wrapped a bearskin carriage rug tenderly about her shoulders. "It is going to get very cold," he said.

His hands stayed on her shoulders as he looked down at her.

He gave an odd little sigh and bent his mouth to hers. At first, it was not like the wild, passionate kisses of Honey's dreams. It was warm and tender and comforting. It felt the most natural thing in the world.

Feeling safe and at home, she put a confiding arm about his neck and kissed him back.

And that was when the dreams became reality as they were both struck by a wave of intense passion. He kissed her until they were both breathless, he kissed her until her lips were bruised, he kissed her with increasing force and passion while the rain drummed down on the carriage roof and the thunder crashed about the heavens.

He pulled her onto his knees so that he could hug her closer. He buried his lips in her hair and then returned to her mouth again, feeling her passion mounting to match his own.

And then his eye caught a movement outside the window and he gently put her from him. The storm had passed as quickly as it had come. The sky was blue and people were beginning to move about outside.

He lifted Honey from his knees and placed her gently on the seat beside him. "My love," he said quickly, "I must tell you before Lady Canon returns. I had a letter from my mother this morning. She is ailing, and I must leave you to go to the country. I will not be gone above a week. Wait for me. Do you understand?"

She nodded dumbly, wanting to say she would

wait for him forever if need be, but too stunned with love to say a word.

The carriage door opened and Lady Canon climbed in.

"There you are!" she said brightly. "The outing is quite ruined because the meadow is sodden. Pray tell your coachman to drive us back to Town."

The journey back was a silent one. Lady Canon was too worried to speak. Honey was staring at Lord Alistair Stewart like a mazed fool. Lady Canon did not recognize the face of love. She only thought Honey was besotted in a stupid way and that Lord Alistair looked half asleep.

Lord Alistair refused her invitation to take tea. He kissed Honey's hand in farewell, and wished Lady Canon would leave them alone together so that he might kiss her good-bye.

Honey floated into the house on Charles Street in a daze of happiness.

"Honoria!" said Lady Canon. "A word with you, *if* you please."

"Certainly," said Honey vaguely, giving her aunt a sweet smile.

Lady Canon fretted and fumed until the tea tray was brought in and the servants dismissed.

"Now," she said, "just what has been happening between you and Lord Alistair?"

Honey laughed. "Is it not wonderful, aunt?

We are in love and we are to be married. Oh, I am the luckiest girl alive!"

"Lord Alistair proposed *marriage*?"

"Not *exactly*, Aunt Elizabeth. But he loves me, and I . . . oh, I love him so very much."

"It is all my fault," said Lady Canon. "The wretched man."

Honey looked amused. "Do not blame yourself, aunt. In fact, accept my thanks. It was you who threw us together."

"I know," said Lady Canon. "But I did not expect a man like Lord Alistair to go this far."

Honey sat very still, fighting down a chill little feeling of dread that was starting up inside her.

"Please explain yourself, aunt."

"I thought you were about to make a fool of yourself over Channington, and so I asked Lord Alistair to attract your attention to himself."

"And he agreed?"

"With great reluctance. I am a good friend of his mama, the Duchess of Bewley, and so I knew he would eventually give in and do it to please me."

"I cannot believe it." Honey felt sick. "He told me to wait for him. He has gone to the country to see the duchess, who is ill."

"Believe me, the Duchess of Bewley has never had a day's illness in her life. He knew he had gone too far, and so he was beating a gentlemanly retreat."

"I was so sure he loved me," whispered Honey.

Again Lady Canon experienced that unrecognized stab of jealousy.

"You are such a widgeon," she said. "You will see the wisdom of it in the weeks to come. Look how easily you became enamored of Lord Alistair. *That* should show you that you must put a guard on your unruly emotions. You are very young."

"He seemed sincere."

"Of course he did," snapped Lady Canon. "He would not have been able to woo you else."

"And you both sat here and plotted the whole thing," said Honey. "You disgust me. Both of you."

"You are understandably bitter. But you will recover. You young things! In another week, you will be just as much in love with someone else." Lady Canon laughed and poured more tea while Honey stared at her with hate-filled eyes.

"I would like to return to Kelidon," she said in a flat voice.

"That would be very selfish of you," said Lady Canon calmly. "Why run away because a man proves false? You must face up to reality. You are living between the pages of circulating library romances. Real life is not thus. Your father has gone to great expense to send you here. You cannot repay him by returning home in a pettish temper. Now, go to your room and bathe your face and you will feel much better. We go to Chumleys' rout tonight."

Honey looked at her in appalled wonder. Her world had smashed and crashed about her ears and yet Aunt Elizabeth went on pouring tea.

Once in her room, Honey lay down on the bed and cried and cried. Her bitter mind distorted every caress until Lord Alistair appeared a jeering, cynical monster.

Somehow she would get her revenge on her aunt, and on Lord Alistair. No, she would not run home to Kelidon. She owed her father a great deal and she would do her best to bring home a husband.

She rose and washed her face and hands and then rang for brandy, ignoring the chambermaid's startled look. The stately Beecham was informed and promptly told Lady Canon that her niece was demanding brandy.

"Let her have it," said Lady Canon wearily. She was beginning to feel very guilty about her treatment of Honey, and the more guilty she felt, the more she became convinced it must all be someone else's fault.

Honey drank several glasses of brandy. Then she allowed herself to be turned and pinned and taped by Clarisse as she was prepared for the rout.

Lord Channington was already at the rout when Honey entered with Lady Canon. Like all womanizers, Lord Channington did not really like women one bit and yet had that strong feminine streak which is part of every Don Juan's make-up which makes him peculiarly susceptible to the changing moods of his prey.

He therefore knew immediately that Honey was in great emotional pain. He had heard all the gossip about how Lord Alistair and Miss Honeyford had been smelling of April and May at the fête in the Surrey fields, and he had heard just as he arrived at the rout of Lord Alistair's sudden departure from town. The cynics were already sniggering that Lord Alistair had escaped the parson's mousetrap as he had done so many times before.

He read the signs of rejection and pain in Honey's face, although to the rest of the company, Miss Honeyford was even more beautiful than she had ever been.

He waited until Lady Canon's attention was engaged and made his way quickly to Honey's side.

"I am charmed to see you in looks, Miss Honeyford," he said.

Honey gave him a glittering, cynical look.

"*Really* charmed to see you," he said, "even

though Lady Canon does not approve of me. I refused to marry the daughter of a friend of hers who was trying to trap me into marriage, and ever since then Lady Canon has put it about that I am a hardened womanizer. What does one do to live down such a reputation, Miss Honeyford?"

"I think by not believing a word that Lady Canon says," said Honey, looking at him for the first time.

"Something has upset you badly," he said in a gentle voice, "and I know all this crush of people is fatiguing you. Do you stay here long?"

"No, fortunately," said Honey. "Aunt Elizabeth has promised me an early night."

"Come riding with me early in the Park," he urged.

"My aunt would not allow it."

"What she does not know will not upset her. You could be back before she awoke."

"The servants would tell her."

"Let them. I am a respectable gentleman and she cannot really do anything to stop you. I have missed you, Miss Honeyford."

His voice was kind, and Honey felt that old sensation of warmth and security. It would be wonderful to have an hour of freedom in the Park with this man who she was beginning to think was the only friend she had in the world. And the very fact that neither her aunt nor

Lord Alistair approved of him gave him an added charm.

"I do not have a horse," she said.

"Give me the pleasure of mounting you," said Lord Channington earnestly—"in every sense," he added to himself.

Honey hesitated. Lady Canon was approaching with a fat and fortyish man on her arm. Honey could tell from the gleam in her eye that Lady Canon felt she had secured an eligible man for Honey. Honey looked at the dull features of the approaching suitor and then up at Lord Channington's strong, handsome face.

"Yes," she whispered urgently. "Be outside the house at seven."

Lord Channington bowed and moved away. Seven o'clock! Dear heavens. He would need to stay awake all night. But the time was ripe for the seduction of Honey. He could see the bitter rage in her eyes, and shrewdly knew she would be prepared to run off with him to spite Lord Alistair Stewart.

Eight

That ride in the Park was the beginning of the healing days for Honey. Lord Channington's warmth, courtesy, and friendship were like balm. The fact that their friendship had to be kept secret from Lady Canon forged a bond between them in the following days.

Lord Channington, for his part, became more and more enamored of Honey and longed to possess her. For the moment, he was happy to play on her bitter, rejected feelings, making her more and more dependent on him for solace.

Lady Canon never found out about that first early morning ride, for Lord Channington had taken the precaution of bribing Beecham heavily, and, since Lady Canon was not the sort of mistress to inspire devotion in any of her servants since she underpaid them shamelessly, Beecham willingly became part of the plot.

Her outings with Lord Channington were kept secret by Beecham and the other servants, and when Lady Canon retired for an afternoon nap, Lord Channington was ushered into the downstairs drawing room to drink tea with Miss Honeyford.

When a week passed and Lord Alistair did not return to London, Honey could only be glad that the wounds were not to be reopened so soon by the sight of him.

A letter with his seal on it arrived for her, but since she was so sure it would be full of patronizing apologies and explanations, she threw it on the fire unopened and watched with grim satisfaction as it flared up and then settled down to a shriveled black mess in the grate. "Just like my love for you, my lord," muttered Honey, seizing the poker and viciously stabbing at the ashes.

Lord Alistair Stewart wandered restlessly around his parents' enormous ducal mansion. His mother had influenza—much to his surprise, because he was used to her manufacturing illnesses—and although her fever had broken and she was now out of danger, his father had begged him to stay for a few more days in order to encourage her back to health.

He had told the duke, his father, of his plans to marry Miss Honeyford, and, since he was not the heir, his father clapped him on the shoulder and said he could marry whom he pleased.

The weather had turned gray and cloudy and the days were long and tedious. He now wished he had stayed in Town long enough to persuade Lady Canon to let him take Honey to the country with him.

At last, he was eventually able to set out for London. He had been away for nine days. He had dreamed of Honey constantly.

He was glad he had never been in love before. He felt he was coming to her new and shining. The long string of mistresses might never have existed. The miles seemed to crawl under his wheels, and he fretted at every delay.

Honey awoke with tears running down her cheeks. She had dreamed all night long of Lord Alistair, dreamed that they were married and secure and happy. More than ever was she determined to banish him from her mind. She longed to see Lord Channington again. His presence was the only thing which eased her hurt and longing.

Lord Alistair had sent his servants ahead the day before his departure to prepare the town house for his arrival and so the news of his impending return reached the ever-alert ears of Lord Channington. He called early at Charles Street to give the gratified Beecham another heavy bribe and a letter for Honey, asking her to meet him in the Green Park at the Piccadilly Gate at ten in the morning.

Lady Canon did not rise before noon and so it was easy for Honey to escape. Her heart sank a little as she saw how serious he looked. He said nothing until they had walked a little way into the park. He drew her under the shadow of a large horse chestnut and took her hands in his, looking intently down into her face.

"We have been seen by that terrible gossiping Osborne female," he lied. "I fear for the end of our friendship."

Tears started to Honey's eyes as she thought of the empty days ahead, days where she would have nothing else to do but torture herself with thoughts of the faithless Lord Alistair.

"What are we to do?" she whispered.

"Get married," he said simply.

"Lady Canon might accept the idea," said Honey. "Her objections surely have been solely on the grounds that you have no intention of every marrying anyone."

"No," he said. "She is a bitter woman, and a bitter woman never forgives!"

That struck such an answering chord in Honey's breast that she could only nod. She never stopped for a moment to wonder whether she should really go ahead and marry Lord Channington. He had become necessary to her. Without him, life would be a hell of hurt and rejection.

"I do not love you," said Honey, "but I could come to love you. I feel I must be honest . . ."

"I *know* you will come to love me," he said passionately.

"But what can I do?"

"It is quite simple. We can steal away tomorrow and stay with my mother at my home in Bedfordshire, and we can get married at our local church."

Honey took a deep breath. "When would we leave?"

"Tomorrow. At dawn. You are not being unfair to Lady Canon. She only wishes you to make a good marriage and so she will gracefully accept our marriage when it is a fait accompli."

"It is very soon," said Honey.

He played his ace.

"Lord Alistair Stewart returns to London tomorrow."

"You know," she whispered.

"I know you have been hurt by him. Yes."

"And you do not care?"

"My love for you is greater than all these petty little considerations."

"Then I will go with you," said Honey in a low voice, "and I consider myself fortunate that I have secured such a good friend as a husband."

Her eyes were large and trusting.

"You must not confide in *anyone*," said Lord Channington, thinking, God forbid she should discover my mother has been dead these five years.

"No, I will not tell anyone," said Honey.

"Lady Canon's servants will not betray you. I have paid Beecham handsomely to be our ally, and he will make sure the rest keep quiet."

"It seems so dishonest," said Honey. "I must at least leave a letter for Aunt Elizabeth."

"No, not even that. She will have a few anxious days and then we will send her an express to tell her the happy news."

He held Honey's hands in a firm clasp. "Until tomorrow."

"Until tomorrow," echoed Honey sadly.

She was very quiet and preoccupied for the rest of the day—which all went to show what a firm hand could do, thought Lady Canon with satisfaction. Soon she and Lord Alistair would be able to laugh together over the silly chit's infatuation.

She was in such a good humor that when Honey pleaded the headache that evening, saying she was unable to go out, Lady Canon agreed it was best she should spend the evening in bed.

Her pleasure in Honey's meek demeanor caused her to fuss over the girl, giving her a tisane and making sure a fire was made up in her room, for the evening had turned unseasonably cold.

All these ministrations made Honey feel guilty. It was a monstrous trick her aunt had played on her, and yet she had done it all from the best motives.

Honey suddenly knew she could not have a quiet conscience unless she left Lady Canon a letter at least explaining that she was leaving Town with Lord Channington. She did not need to go so far as to say where she could be found.

She wrote a very short letter saying that since she was sure Lady Canon would never permit the marriage, she had decided to go away with Lord Channington and be married quietly out of Town. She thanked her aunt for all her kindness and begged her forgiveness.

Honey then packed the clothes she had brought with her when she had arrived in London. All the beautiful gowns were part of her disastrous love for Lord Alistair. She wanted to take nothing with her to remind her of any time she had danced with him, any time she had even looked at him.

She sat huddled in a chair beside the fire, waiting for the dawn, frightened to sleep lest she should not wake in time, and frightened to sleep in case she dreamed once more of Lord Alistair and that the dream might weaken her resolve.

Honey no longer knew who she was. The Honey of the hunting field had ridden off never to return. The belle of the London Season also seemed a shadowy figure. She felt young and defenseless and very alone.

Her eyes drooped and closed. She was running down a long avenue and Lord Alistair was pursuing her. He was shouting something, but she put her hands over her ears as she ran. He was coming nearer and nearer. She tripped over a stone in the road and woke with a start.

The dream seemed to have lasted a minute, but the watch outside was calling hoarsely that it was six-thirty and a fine morning.

Honey drew back the curtains and yellow sunlight flooded the room. Her spirits lifted. She was leaving all the shame and humiliation of London behind.

A new life awaited her.

From now on, she would only look forward.

She picked up her two small valises and her old sacklike reticule and crept down the shadowy stairs where Sir Angus Canon's far-from-illustrious ancestors coldly watched her escape with their painted eyes from the portraits lining the walls of the staircase.

The house had a listening air as she opened the front door and slipped quietly outside.

"There she goes," said Beecham to the maid, Clarisse, as they watched from an upstairs window.

"I hope milady does not blame us," said Clarisse, peering down at the small figure standing on the step.

"Lady Canon does not see us as human beings," said Beecham. "She will not guess we had anything to do with the matter."

To Honey's relief, a closed carriage came along Charles Street and stopped in front of her. Lord Channington opened the door and sprang lightly down onto the road.

"Come, my bride," he said.

Honey felt suddenly and inexplicably afraid. She turned and looked up at the house, but there was nothing to be seen but blank windows since Clarisse and Beecham had quickly retired behind a curtain.

Honey gave a little sigh. She let him help her into the carriage.

The coachman cracked his whip and they set off in the direction of Piccadilly at a smart pace.

Honey felt awkward at being shut up in the intimacy of the carriage with Lord Channington, but he smiled at her and begged her permission to allow him to sleep. Soon Honey fell asleep herself.

She awoke when they rolled up to the posting inn in Barnet. They stopped for refreshment, Honey enjoying the ease created by being escorted by this rich and titled earl. The best table was laid for them, and the host and an army of servants hovered about.

She was grateful to Lord Channington for chatting on as if they were riding in the Park, instead of eloping. He talked social nonsense, telling her who had been at White's the night before and which man had lost a fortune and which man had won an estate.

When they were back in the carriage, he leaned forward and kissed her lightly on the cheek, but it was a brotherly caress.

Lord Channington had been up most of the night gambling and so he soon fell asleep again.

It was a beautiful day. Sunny fields and cottages rolled past and the well-sprung coach swept onward up the road to Bedfordshire.

Honey hoped Lord Channington's mother would not be too shocked, and began to regret having left her fine clothes behind.

And then she thought of Lord Alistair. He was so close to her it was as if he was in the carriage. He was furious. He hated her.

Honey screwed her eyes up tightly, but the

tears forced their way through her lids and trickled down her cheeks.

Lord Alistair was going to ask Lady Canon's permission to pay his addresses to Honey. He felt ridiculously young as he washed and changed into his best clothes.

Lady Canon had just finishing dressing when Beecham climbed the stairs to announce his arrival. She turned a faint pink, and shouted to Clarisse to lay out the best silk. Hurry!

She would tease Lord Alistair a little, she thought, about his success in ensnaring Honey, but she would also lecture him for having gone too far.

Lady Canon had not felt so young or so feminine in years as she descended from the bedroom to the saloon amid a rustle of expensive silk. She paused outside the door of the saloon and adjusted her becoming lace cap in the mirror.

Lord Alistair rose to meet her as she entered the room with such a radiant smile on his face that her heart began to beat very hard and her breathing became rapid.

"Where is she?" asked Lord Alistair. Then he laughed, a great joyous laugh. "Only see how impatient I am, Lady Canon. I am supposed to beg your permission first, and yet I cannot wait to see her."

Lady Canon paused and put a faltering hand to her mouth.

"Who? What? Do you wish to see *Honey*? But that farce is ended, my lord."

"The farce has most certainly ended," he said cheerfully, "and real life is about to begin. Poor Lady Canon. You must think my wits are wandering. Did not Honoria tell you? We are to be married."

"Married!" Lady Canon put out a trembling hand and supported herself on the back of a chair.

"Yes," he said. "May I see her?"

"Of course," said Lady Canon weakly. The incredible had happened. Lord Alistair Stewart was getting married at last. She rang the bell and then wondered whether to tell Lord Alistair of Honey's shock when she had told her he had only courted her because he had been asked to woo her away from Channington.

But Beecham answered the bell promptly.

"Tell Miss Honeyford that Lord Alistair is anxious to see her," said Lady Canon.

Beecham stood very still without moving. Lord Alistair read apprehension in the butler's face and added sharply, "Well, go and fetch her."

Beecham turned and walked stiffly from the room. Now was Lady Canon's opportunity to tell Lord Alistair what she had told Honey, but she looked at his glowing face and found she could not.

She felt old and ugly. The man in front of her did not see her was a woman, but only as his beloved's elderly relative.

"How is your dear mama?" she asked through dry lips.

"Much better, I thank you. She had the influenza. I was amazed when I arrived to find she was really ill. You know how it is, being an old friend of hers, she often *makes* herself ill, but this time it was genuine. I was glad I went, although I wish I had had the foresight to beg you to let me take Honoria with me."

"Yes," said Lady Canon dully.

There was a long silence. Lord Alistair did not seem to notice. He was quite obviously straining his ears to hear Honey's step on the stair outside.

At last Beecham opened the door and stood just inside as if prepared for flight.

"Miss Honeyford is not in her room," he said. "There was only this letter addressed to you, my lady."

Lady Canon opened the letter and read it several times, as if willing the contents to change to something different.

"Very good, Beecham," she said. "That will be all."

Beecham bowed and withdrew, closing the doors behind him.

"What is it?" demanded Lord Alistair sharply. Lady Canon wordlessly held out the letter to him. Lord Alistair read it. He suddenly looked older, harsher. Lady Canon felt as if she had never really understood the passions that could wrack the human breast before. She looked at the torment in Lord Alistair's eyes with a kind of dazed wonder.

"Was she here last night?" he demanded.

"Oh, yes," faltered Lady Canon. "She said she had the headache and I put her to bed myself."

"Then she either left during the night or early this morning."

"I don't know," said Lady Canon wretchedly. "I do not see what we can do. She says in her letter that she and Channington are to be married, so we may as well make the best of things."

"If Channington marries her, then it will be a miracle. If she is married by the time I get my hands on them, then she will shortly be a widow."

"My dear Lord Alistair, you are becoming overexercised—"

"Your servants must have known," he interrupted.

Lady Canon drew herself up. "My servants would not go against my interests. Only see how concerned Beecham was when Miss Honeyford went to the hanging."

"Has Beecham been with you long?"

"He came to me as a footman when my husband was alive. He has been my butler for twenty-five years."

"During which time he has had many increases in salary?"

"His pay was naturally increased when he became butler."

"But not since then."

"Of course not. I do not see what this has to—"

"Good day to you, Lady Canon."

"Lord Alistair, what am I going to do about Honoria?"

"Pray," he said savagely.

Lord Alistair saw Beecham hovering at the foot of the stairs.

"Beecham," he said, "I am not going to waste time with accusations and recriminations. My Lord Channington greased your hand heavily to aid and abet him. I know this, so there is no point in lying. Unless you want me to persuade Lady Canon of this, and have you turned off without a character, you will tell me when she left."

Beecham looked at Lord Alistair's implacable face. "I could not help myself, my lord," he said. "I asked my lady for more money a month ago and she refused. She said butlers were ten a penny and I should consider myself lucky to have a roof over my head. Lord Channington gave me enough to settle my debts and to pay the other servants for their silence. He is very much in love with Miss Honeyford, and he is an earl, and it didn't seem wrong to help him."

"When did she leave?" demanded Lord Alistair.

"This very morning, just before seven. She went off in a closed carriage with Lord Channington."

Lord Alistair walked past him and out into the street. His grain was in a turmoil. She *could not* be in love with Channington. Why? Why had she left? Even if Lady Canon had told her about the plot to woo her away from Channington, she must have received his letter, and would know he planned to marry her. But what if she had not received his letter?

Channington did not mean marriage. His estates lay to the north of Bedfordshire. He might head in that direction to reassure her he meant to marry her from his home.

He must find her. He could not bear it if she returned to town as quiet and broken as Pamela Hudson had been. It was hard to imagine Honey being seduced by such as Channington. He decided to ride north in pursuit. He would not take his carriage. He would go on horse-back and hunt them down.

Once at his town house, he changed into riding clothes, and had his servants put a change of clothes in his saddle bags, along with a pair of pistols.

And then he rode like the wind.

He decided to change his horse as frequently as possible, and to cut across country where the road took too many turns and twists.

He had his first news of them at Barnet and changed his horse for a great rangy hunter and set out without even pausing to eat or drink.

Although they had had a long start on him, they were obviously making a leisurely journey. He had news of them again at St. Alban's and rode doggedly ahead, a picture of Honey always before his mind's eye.

And then, as night closed in, he lost track of them. Precious time was lost doubling back on the road. He was tired and hungry and worried to death. He stopped the Royal Mail to ask about posting houses in the area and nearly had his head blown off by the terrified driver, who thought he was a highwayman.

But when the driver calmed down, he proved to be a useful source of information. He was a Luton man and knew of a new inn called The Goat in Boots which stood a little way off the road, about eight miles ahead.

It had become so firmly fixed in his mind that they would be there that he could hardly believe his ears when the landlord told him he had never heard of or seen such a couple. He gave Lord Alistair a list of posting houses and inns in the neighborhood together with directions to them all.

Lord Alistair's horse was weary. He had to find a good posting inn in order to get a fresh one, for he meant to search all night if need be.

The night was very dark and a thin drizzle had started to fall.

He was riding through a small dark wood which edged either side of the road when two dark figures plunged out of the trees.

"Stand and deliver," said a hoarse voice.

Lord Alistair's first weary thought was, "Why, tonight of all nights?" He had never been held up by highwaymen before, although he had spent a great deal of time on the roads of England.

He studied the two men. He could not make out whether they were armed with pistols or not, but he decided it safer to assume they were.

He swung down from his horse and faced them.

"Stand over there," growled one. "Bring us the glim," the robber said to his companion, "and we'll see what we have here."

Lord Alistair stood in the rain, dejected and weary. Then he remembered that in one of his saddle bags was a ruby ring which he had bought for Honey. All at once he knew they must not touch that ring.

From being a menace, the two robbers became a nuisance standing between him and his beloved.

Quick as lightning he sprang straight at the man who was covering him with a pistol—or what he assumed was a pistol. He lashed out in the dark and smashed his fist down onto the man's arm. There was an explosion as a gun went off. He slammed his fist into the man's face. His eyes were now accustomed to the blackness, and he neatly jumped sideways and ducked as a cudgel wielded by the other robber whizzed harmlessly past his head. He punched the second man in the kidneys and then, in a mad rage, picked him up bodily and threw him full at the first, who was just struggling to his feet.

Lord Alistair mounted his horse and set off down the road at a gallop.

By the time the lights of the next town began to flicker through the trees, Lord Alistair Stewart was praying hard that he might find Miss Honeyford and Lord Channington soon while he still had the strength to strangle the one and to shoot the other.

* * *

Honey sat in front of the glass in the best bedroom that The King's Head had to offer and studied her reflection. Care and worry did not seem to have aged her in the least. Her skin was smooth, her color was good, and her now longer hair shone with health.

She was glad to be on her own for a little. Lord Channington's behavior had been faultless. He could have been taking her for an outing in the Park instead of eloping with her. But Honey was uneasy. She decided she must be tired. That would surely explain her increasing uneasiness.

The King's Head stood a little outside Leighton Buzzard. Honey had expected they would press on to Luton and had a feeling that Leighton Buzzard was surely out of their way. But Lord Channington had obviously stayed at this inn before. The landlord had hailed him as an honored guest and had promised the best bedroom for my lord's "sister." The news that she was to masquerade as his sister and that she was to have a separate bedchamber filled her with—what she privately thought as disproportionate—relief. And yet Lord Channington had done nothing to even hint he would expect any intimacy before marriage.

Honey thought of Lord Alistair. It was like having a death in the family. Time would heal the wound and by the time she saw him again it was more than likely she would be amazed that she had ever fancied herself to be in love with him.

She had put on the brown silk gown, finding to her dismay that these old clothes she had worn for the journey to London evoked more memories of Lord Alistair than any of her new finery would have done.

The inn was very quiet. The stone-mullioned windows, the rich oak cornices, and the wainscoted corridors showed the old building's Tudor origin. Like so many other inns, it was probably called The Pope's Head at one time and had had its name changed at the time of King Henry the Eighth in order to save the landlord from losing his own head.

Honey tidied her hair again. She was reluctant to go downstairs to join Lord Channington in the dining room. Now that she was on the road, now that she had left London behind, a little voice in her head was beginning to accuse her of being too precipitate. She raised the hairbrush again and her hand stopped in midair. She had been very ready to believe Lady Canon. What if . . . just supposing that Lord Alistair had set out to woo her on Lady Canon's instructions and then found himself in love?

But that was ridiculous. Lady Canon was an

eminently practical woman. If there had been
any hope of her niece's marrying the son of a
duke, then she would have encouraged Honey
for all she was worth.

Honey sighed and put down the hairbrush.
The most comforting thing she could do was to
live entirely in the minute, neither mourning
yesterday or dreading the morrow.

Honey made her way downstairs at last, feeling more at ease.

Lord Channington jumped to his feet as soon
as she entered the dining room. He pulled out
a chair for her and then seized her hand and
kissed it.

"You should not do that," whispered Honey
fiercely, her eyes on the waiter. "I am supposed to be your sister."

"Of course you are, my love," said Lord
Channington gaily. "I had forgot."

After all, Honey was not to know she was by
no means the first "sister" he had brought to
this inn.

He sat down opposite her and poured her a
glass of wine. He eyed her covertly as she
shook out her napkin. What a dreadful gown!
Leighton Buzzard was still conveniently close
to Town. He would have her this very night,
and if she pleasured him well, he might consider keeping her for a little. But it was the
initial seduction of a female which was more

important to Lord Channington than the love-making itself. Once the prize was won, he soon lost interest.

"If we make good time," he realized Honey was saying, "we should reach your home to-morrow. I hope your mother will not be put out by my visit and the announcement of our marriage."

"Nothing in the world ever shocks and disturbs my mother," laughed Lord Channington, and since that good lady was reposing in the family vault, he spoke nothing but the truth.

"There will be a lot of explaining to do," said Honey. "She will wonder at my not having a maid. She will wonder why we ran away together instead of staying in London."

"Don't worry about it," said Lord Channington. "Have some more burgundy. The landlord keeps an excellent cellar."

Their food arrived and they ate in silence. Lord Channington was pleased to see that Honey was drinking a lot of wine.

Honey looked around once the cover had been cleared and noticed that they were alone in the dining room.

"Are you in love with me, my lord?" she asked abruptly.

"My love," he said, "how can you ask such a thing? I have never loved any woman the way I love you."

Honey found herself wishing his eyes would show more what he was thinking and feeling. But his dead brown eyes observed her steadily although his mouth smiled.

Again, Honey experienced that feeling of unease. All at once she wanted to be alone, but put her nervousness down to fatigue.

"My apologies," she said, rising to her feet. "I must retire."

"By all means, my sweeting. We are both anxious for bed."

Was it a trick of the candlelight or did his eyes gleam with a reddish light?

"At what time do we leave in the morning?" asked Honey.

"I will get the chambermaid to call you in plenty of time," said Lord Channington, who had, in fact, told the landlord not to disturb them. But he had to admit to himself that he had drunk too much and he did not feel energetic enough to begin the siege of Honey.

She hesitated. "I have something on my conscience," she said.

"My love?"

"I know I promised you I would not tell anyone, and I did not, in a way."

He sat down and carefully poured himself a glass of port, tipping the glass idly backward and forward and watching the heavy drops of liquid cling to the sides.

"Go on," he said softly.

"I did not tell you all about ... about Lord Alistair."

The deuce! he thought. Never tell me Stewart has had her first.

Honey sat down again. She rested her chin on her hands. "It was like this," she said. "Lord Alistair was courting me, most assiduously. He led me to believe he had marriage in mind."

"Odd's Noddikins," drawled Lord Channington. "He always does."

"Lady Canon then told me she had asked him to court me so as to divert my attention from you."

"And?"

"And after that, I naturally wished never to see Lord Alistair again."

"Quite right," said Lord Channington. "Is that all that is on your conscience?"

"No-o. You see, the previous evening, because I wanted to pack, I told Lady Canon I had the headache. She surprised me by being most kind and solicitous. I hated her, you see, for conniving with Lord Alistair. I felt betrayed. But I began to realize she has not much understanding of the softer feelings. I do not think she has ever been in love. She had done her best to puff me off in society and has, I believe, gone to a great deal of personal expense."

"And so?" asked Lord Channington, trying to stifle a cavernous yawn.

"And so I left her a letter."

"The devil you did!"

"I did not tell her where I was to be found," pleaded Honey. "I only said I was leaving with you and that we were to be married."

Lord Channington briefly closed his eyes. Already coaches full of enraged people could be scouring the countryside for them. If he was going to have this chit, it would need to be tonight or never.

He forced himself to smile. "Do not look so worried, my darling," he said. "Go to your room and do not worry about anything. I am here to take care of you."

Honey gave him a watery smile. "There are times when I think you are *much* too good for me."

She rose to her feet and leaned forward and gave him a quick kiss on the cheek.

Honey left the dining room and crossed the hall to the staircase. The landlord bowed low before her. "Goodnight, my lady," he said, and to Honey's amazement one of the landlord's eyelids dropped in a fat wink.

She went up the stairs, feeling puzzled. Why had the man been so rude and familiar? But she was so tired, too tired to think any more.

She would complain to Lord Channington about the landlord in the morning.

But the innkeeper's insolence made her feel nervous. She undressed and brushed out her hair, tied a nightcap on top of her curls, and climbed into bed. She blew out the candle beside the bed but left the rushlight burning in its pierced cannister. After she had been lying for some moments, she got up again and took the pistol out of her reticule, primed it, and put it under her pillow. Then she turned on her side and composed herself for sleep.

Suddenly there came a scratching at the door.

She stiffened. Perhaps it was the landlord. Perhaps the overly familiar landlord was drunk. She drew the pistol out and, holding it firmly in her hand, called out, "Who is there?"

The door swung open and Lord Channington strolled into the room in all the glory of a cambric nightshirt and a red Kilmarnock nightcap.

She was jerked toward him, her feet slipped on the polished boards, she shot down and through his legs, twisted around, and turned and fired.

There was a terrific explosion and Lord Channington screamed and clutched his left buttock.

"She shot me. Help! Help! Murder!" he roared.

Downstairs, the landlord was just climbing into bed when the loud commotion from the best bedchamber came to his ears. He hesitated. But my lord had been most insistent that he was not to be disturbed. The landlord pulled his nightcap down around his ears and got into bed.

Lord Channington threw himself face-down on Honey's bed, still howling for help.

"Get to your own room, sirrah," said Honey. She reloaded her pistol and held it to the side of his head.

He twisted about and stared straight up into Honey's implacable eyes.

Somehow he got himself from the bed and walked to the door with Honey following close behind.

His room was next to Honey's. He tried to shut the door on her, but she pushed her way in behind him. The back of Lord Channington's nightshirt was stained with blood and blood dripped on to the floor.

Honey felt herself growing faint. But there was one thing she had to make him do before she ran for help.

"You will write a letter, Lord Channington," she said grimly. "It is only a few lines. I will dictate them. When you have finished, I will send for the surgeon. Do you understand?"

"Anything," wailed Lord Channington. "Oh, hurry. I am dying."

He stood in front of the writing desk and pulled forward a sheet of paper.

"I, the Earl of Channington," said Honey, "do hereby state that I came by the wound in my left buttock when cleaning my pistol. I laid it on the floor and stood on it by accident, and it went off. I am shortly to be married to Miss Honoria Honeyford who resides with me at this inn, and who will handle all my affairs until such time as I am fit to take control of them myself.

"Good," said Honey, when he had signed the paper. "I have no mind to hang. My father wishes me to bring home a husband, and that husband is going to be you, my lord. Get into bed and I will fetch a surgeon."

She hurried from the room, taking the key with her, and locking Lord Channington in.

Once in the corridor, she leaned her head against the wall and shivered violently. It was a few moments before she could compose herself enough to make her way downstairs.

She picked up the handbell by the door of the inn and rang it violently. The landlord would appear soon enough if he thought he had a new customer.

He blinked when he saw himself faced with a trembling girl clad only in a nightdress and holding a pistol.

In a cold, calm voice, Honey explained what had happened, or rather, what she wished the landlord and the rest of the world to believe had happened.

"Are there any other guests here?" asked Honey.

The landlord shook his head. "My lord bought up all the rooms," he said, shaking his dazed head to clear it, "so I gave the rest of the guests their marching orders."

"Then you will not allow any other guest to stay here until I tell you," said Honey. "We will cease this fiction about my being my lord's sister. I am his fiancée, Miss Honeyford. Do you understand?"

The landlord nodded, eyeing the pistol warily.

"Then be off with you," said Honey, "and send a servant to my lord's bedchamber with hot water, towels, and laudanum."

Honey forced herself to walk back up the stairs. She must not give way to weak and missish feelings. Lord Channington must not die.

She unlocked his room. He was lying face-down on the bed and twisted his head when she entered and looked at her. Honey wondered how she could ever have thought his brown eyes expressionless. They were filled with fear.

"The surgeon is coming," she said. "Now let me have a look at that wound."

"Have you no delicacy?" he screamed. "You are a monster."

"Why so coy now, my lord," said Honey, advancing on the bed. "If you had had your way, I would have been mother-naked myself."

She whipped up his nightshirt and studied the wound, which was a mess of blood. She soaked a towel in warm water and gently bathed it.

She let out a little sigh of relief. "I think you will live," she said.

Lord Channington buried his face in the pillows and moaned.

There was a knock at the door. Honey carefully arranged Lord Channington's nightshirt and went to admit two scared and nervous servants carrying towels, hot water, and laudanum.

Honey poured a generous measure of laudanum in a glass and held it to Lord Channington's lips. "You are going to poison me," he whispered feebly, but he drank it nonetheless.

Honey dismissed the servants and sat down to wait. She felt nothing but contempt for Lord Channington. With a feeling of shock she realized Lord Alistair and Lady Canon had spoken the truth. They *had* been trying to protect her. But Lord Alistair should never have pretended to be in love with her.

Honey was very sure she would never love anyone else as she had loved Lord Alistair. It therefore followed that any husband would do. So Lord Channington would find himself at the altar at Kelidon church just as soon as she could get him there.

It might even be possible to make something of him, thought Honey, hiding in naive dreams from the reality of the fact that she had just shot a man.

Lord Alistair Stewart was almost at the end of his tether. He had searched and searched and he was starving and bone weary.

He had tracked the carriage with the crest on its panel to this neighborhood outside Leighton Buzzard. He had been told by a night traveler that The King's Head was a mile along the road.

After the incident with the highwaymen, his senses were alert to any possibility of danger and he eased a long dueling pistol out of his saddle bag as two dark figures rode toward him from a side road.

The moon had come out from behind the clouds and he saw clearly two men, one dressed like a physician and accompanied by a burly man.

He hailed them and demanded to know if The King's Head was indeed on the road he was traveling.

They reined in beside him. "I am Joseph Benskin, the landlord," said the burly man, "but there ain't no beds on account of a genleman having bespoke all the rooms in the inn."

"Is his name Channington, by any chance?" asked Lord Alistair. "And does he have a Miss Honeyford with him?"

There was a silence. Then, "Better be getting on," muttered Mr. Benskin.

Lord Alistair raised his pistol and pointed it at the landlord.

"Hold!" cried the physician. "There has been enough shooting for one night."

"Shooting?"

"Yes. Allow me to introduce myself. Dr. Bradfield at your service. A gentleman has been shot at the inn and I must get to him as quickly as possible."

"And it *is* Channington," burst out Mr. Benskin, "so for the love of God, let us be on our way."

"Ah!" Lord Alistair let out a long sigh and lowered his gun. "Take me with you," he said. "I know both Lord Channington and Miss Honeyford."

As they rode on, his relief was short-lived. He remembered the pistol Honey always carried. If she had shot Channington, then it would take all his skill to stop her from being hanged.

Lord Alistair had envisioned many meetings with Honey, but never one like this. They went straight up to Lord Channington's bedchamber and pushed open the door. Lord Channington was lying face-down on the bed, snoring stertorously. Honey sat in a chair beside the bed.

At first she thought she was dreaming and that Lord Alistair had come to haunt her. His riding clothes were mud-spattered and his face was drawn and grim.

"What happened?" he asked, desperate to find some way to stop Honey from being dragged off to prison.

"It was an accident," said Honey. "My lord left his gun on the floor and stepped on it by accident. It went off and shot him."

Lord Alistair walked forward and picked up the pistol from the bedside table. He recognized it as Honey's.

"Is this the weapon?"

"Yes."

"Yes, I recognize it as Channington's," lied Lord Alistair.

"Lord Channington was most kind. He is a very brave man," said Honey. "He wrote a letter exonerating me before he collapsed."

"That's a mercy," said Mr. Benskin, who was holding a bowl of water for the doctor. "No need to call the magistrate."

"And he will live," said Dr. Bradfield. "You did a good job of cleaning the wound, Mr. Benskin."

"Wasn't me," said the landlord.

"Thank you, doctor," said Honey quietly. "I cleaned the wound."

"You are a very brave lady," said Dr. Bradfield, looking at her with approval.

"I gave him laudanum," said Honey, "which is why he is sleeping so heavily."

"Good. Good. Now . . . er . . ."

"Miss Honeyford."

"Now Miss Honeyford, I am about to extract the ball. You may retire. I have enough help."

Honey left the room without looking at Lord Alistair.

Lord Alistair felt immeasurably tired. It had been an accident. And so familiar was Miss Honeyford with Channington that she had bathed his wound.

Nine

The morning dawned bright and glorious, but both Honey and Lord Alistair slept like the dead in their respective rooms.

It was eleven o'clock in the morning when Honey eventually made her way downstairs. She ate a large breakfast and went to sit in the inn garden.

It was very peaceful. The first roses were scenting the air and the long leaves of a willow dappled the grass with moving patterns of light and shade.

The first thing that struck her was that Lord Alistair had ridden in search for her. The second was that Lady Canon had coerced him into it.

He would no doubt shortly arrive on the scene to bully and lecture her and try to force her to go back to London.

But she would not!

She was determined to take Lord Channington home to Kelidon with her, even if it meant holding a pistol to his head for the rest of the journey.

A shadow fell across the grass and she looked up into the steady blue eyes of Lord Alistair. Her lips twisted in a wry smile.

"Men were deceivers ever," she said.

"And a good few women, too," he said, sitting down next to her. "I took a look at your beloved. He is sleeping like a pig and has no fever."

"How soon will we be able to travel?"

"You mean to go through with this? Channington will not marry you."

"Oh, yes he will," said Honey grimly.

"Before I wring your neck, you had better tell me *exactly* what happened."

"Why not?" Honey shrugged. "It is all very simple. After Lady Canon told me that you had merely been following her instructions before fleeing to the country to escape the consequences of your wooing, Lord Channington asked me to elope with him.

"I liked him and trusted him. I had promised myself to bring my father home a good husband. Lord Channington said we were to stay with his mother and be married from there."

"Channington's mother died five years ago, or thereabouts."

"Oh." Honey did not look in the least surprised. "Our journey went very well until last night, when he appeared in my bedchamber. He tried to rip my nightgown, but it would not tear and the force of the pull made my feet slip on the boards. I fell down and slid between his legs. I was holding my pistol and so I shot him."

"Right in the bum."

"Yes, as you so crudely put it."

"But at least he had the gallantry to write that letter."

"Not he. I forced him at pistol point to write it."

"But you cannot possibly want to marry such a man."

"Any man will do," said Honey wearily. "Why go back to London to sit waving my fan in hot rooms, hunting feverishly for a husband? I do not care who I marry."

"Miss Honeyford, did you receive my letter?"

"Oh, yes. That. I burned it without reading it."

"Why?"

"Because you had only pretended to love me."

"Miss Honeyford, I have ridden hard and searched well to find you. I have been attacked by highwaymen. I am still exhausted. What do

I have to do to convince you I love you? Shoot myself?"

"You are funning."

"The deuce! I am sound in wind and limb. Does your father only look kindly on seducers and wastrels?"

"You cannot want to marry me," said Honey, not daring to believe him. "We would have to return to Kelidon. My father needs a man to help him with the land."

"My love, you never asked me what I was doing so far north when we first met on the road. I had been spending some time with an old friend just north of Kelidon, advising *him* how to put his land in good heart."

"I cannot imagine you doing anything so energetic," said Honey, for Lord Alistair was restored to his former glory, having bathed and changed into morning dress.

"I can be very energetic. I can even take you to Kelidon and arrange a special license."

Honey began to tremble. "Do you *really* want to marry me?"

He leaned over and lifted her out of her chair and placed her on his knees.

"Kiss me, Honoria," he said.

"My friends call me Honey."

"Then kiss me, Honey."

Honey screwed up her eyes and pursed her lips, frightened she might find that the old magic had gone. But no sooner had his mouth covered her own than she was swept back to that magical country where passion made time stand still.

"We must wait until poor Lord Channington has recovered," she said when she could.

"Forget Channington, he is not like to die."

"Perhaps I may have reformed him," said Honey earnestly.

"No, I think not. Once the wound to his pride and his bottom heals, he will find some other female to seduce and as quickly as possible."

"But we cannot travel north on horseback?"

"Quite right. We will take Channington's carriage. Since you will have to stay with me unchaperoned at every inn on the road to Kelidon, you will be so sadly compromised by the time we arrive that you will have to marry me."

"Alistair," said Honey, burying her face in his waistcoat, "I do not think I can permit . . . until we are married, I do not think . . ."

He laughed and raised her chin and smiled down into her eyes. "I can wait," he said. "With very great difficulty, I can wait, although it will be sweet torture. Kiss me again."

A few hours later, Lord Channington petulantly tugged the bellrope and demanded to see Mr. Benskin.

"Where is everybody?" he demanded when the landlord entered the room. "I could have died."

"Now, now," said Mr. Benskin soothingly, "Dr. Bradfield said he would call."

"Where is my sister . . . I mean Miss Honeyford?"

"Her's left."

"That's a mercy. Good riddance to a hellcat. The sooner I return to London the better. I will need a team of fresh horses . . ."

"Begging your pardon, my lord, but that other gen'leman, Lord Alistair, he and miss has taken your carriage."

"She is not a woman," said Lord Channington passionately. "She is a witch, a monster, a harpie . . ."

Mr. Benskin bowed his way out of the room, leaving Lord Channington cursing and raving.

Three months later, Lord Alistair was lying in bed, reading his correspondence. Beside him, fast asleep, lay his wife.

He opened a letter from Lady Canon and his eyebrows went up in surprise as he read its contents.

He nudged Honey with his elbow. "Wake up, my love. Tremendous news."

Honey came sleepily awake. As she struggled up against the pillows, her flimsy nightdress strained against her breasts. Lord Alistair sighed with pleasure, threw the letter on the floor, and gathered his wife into his arms.

An hour later, Honey asked sleepily, "Why did you wake me?"

"I forget," he whispered against her hair. "Oh, I remember. There is news of Channington."

"What has happened to him?"

"He is to be married."

"There you are," said Honey proudly. "The shock of his attempted elopement with me must have reformed him."

"Not a bit of it. It only started a run of bad luck for him. Lady Canon says he was paying assiduous court to a Miss Teesdale. He was trying his old ploy of proposing to her before persuading her to elope with him. He had bribed the servants to let him into the house while the rest of the family were out. But the Teesdales treat their servants well. So when Lord Channington was down on his knees, the whole family burst out from behind screens in the drawing room where they had been hiding and welcomed him to the bosom of the family."

"Poor Miss Teesdale."

"She evidently knew all about Lord Channington, according to Lady Canon, and *she* set the plot to trap *him*. She has four enormous brothers who are all in the guards. They have promised her she will marry Channington."

Honey began to laugh, her ruffled chestnut curls glinting in the morning sun, and her besotted husband found the sight so enchanting that he thought it would be a very good idea to make love to her again.

About the Author

Born in Glasgow, Scotland, Ms. Chesney started her writing career while working as a fiction buyer in a bookstore in Glasgow. She doubled as a theater critic, newspaper reporter, and editor before coming to the United States in 1971. She later returned to London, where she lives with her husband and one child near Kensington Palace.

Other Regency Romances from SIGNET

(0451)

☐ THE INCORRIGIBLE RAKE by Sheila Walsh. (131940—$2.50)*
☐ THE DIAMOND WATERFALL by Sheila Walsh. (128753—$2.25)*
☐ A SUITABLE MATCH by Sheila Walsh. (117735—$2.25)*
☐ THE RUNAWAY BRIDE by Sheila Walsh. (125142—$2.25)*
☐ A HIGHLY RESPECTABLE MARRIAGE by Sheila Walsh. (118308—$2.25)*
☐ THE INCOMPARABLE MISS BRADY by Sheila Walsh. (092457—$1.75)*
☐ THE ROSE DOMINO by Sheila Walsh. (110773—$2.25)*
☐ THE AMERICAN BRIDE by Megan Daniel. (124812—$2.25)*
☐ THE UNLIKELY RIVALS by Megan Daniel. (110765—$2.25)*
☐ THE SENSIBLE COURTSHIP by Megan Daniel. (117395—$2.25)*
☐ THE RELUCTANT SUITOR by Megan Daniel. (096711—$1.95)*
☐ AMELIA by Megan Daniel. (094875—$1.75)*

*Prices slightly higher in Canada·

Buy them at your local

bookstore or use coupon

on next page for ordering.

SIGNET Regency Romances You'll Enjoy

JOIN THE *REGENCY ROMANCE* READERS' PANEL

Help us bring you more of the books you like by filling out this survey and mailing it in today.

1. Book Title: _____

   Book #: _____

2. Using the scale below, how would you rate this book on the following features? Please write in one rating from 0-10 for each feature in the spaces provided.

POOR	NOT SO GOOD		O.K.			GOOD		EXCEL-LENT	
0	1	2	3	4	5	6	7	8	9	10

                                                                    RATING

Overall opinion of book .... _____
Plot/Story .... _____
Setting/Location .... _____
Writing Style .... _____
Character Development .... _____
Conclusion/Ending .... _____
Scene on Front Cover .... _____

3. About how many romance books do you buy for yourself each month? _____

4. How would you classify yourself as a reader of Regency romances?
   I am a ( ) light ( ) medium ( ) heavy reader.

5. What is your education?
   ( ) High School (or less)   ( ) 4 yrs. college
   ( ) 2 yrs. college   ( ) Post Graduate

6. Age _____   7. Sex: ( ) Male ( ) Female

Please Print Name_____

Address_____

City _____ State _____ Zip _____

Phone # (____)_____

Thank you. Please send to New American Library, Research Dept., 1633 Broadway, New York, NY 10019.